CW01425817

Life
Unwritten

T.I. LOWE

Copyright © 2016 T.I. LOWE

All rights reserved.

ISBN: 9781674048901

DEDICATION

To every person struggling with body image. Strive to be the best person you can be, never allowing someone else the power of measuring your self-worth. Go out there and claim the life God has written for you to live.

BOOKS BY T.I. LOWE

Lulu's Café
Goodbyes & Second Chances
A Bleu Streak Christmas
A Bleu Streak Summer
Coming Home Again
Julia's Journey
A Discovery of Hope
Any Given Moment
Orange Blossom Café
Until I Do
Until I Don't
Until I Decide
Beach Haven
Driftwood Dreams
Sea Glass Castle

ACKNOWLEDGMENTS

A special thank you to my lovely readers. Your enthusiasm over my stories and unwavering support touches my heart more than I can express in words. My honest and dependable beta readers, Sally Anderson, Trina Cooke, Lynn Edge, Linda Saylor, and Jennifer Strickland.

Thanks for your guidance in making this story better.

My Lowe family, Bernie, Nate, and Lydia.

You make my life brighter and sweeter. Love ya!

My Savior Jesus Christ, thank You for being the lamp to my feet and the light to this blessed writing path.

Chapter One

"I have lost my ever-loving mind." The words whisper out through my clenched teeth as I glare at my decision to go all the way this time. If I ever decide to do something, it's all the way, baby, or not at all. Such a bad habit…

"Get the lead out," a big guy barks out from where he stands in front of a few dozen more idiots as I scoot off my golf cart. Mr. Hunk of Man wears a whistle around his thick neck that intermingles with a set of authentic military dog tags, making it easy to guess he is my worst nightmare.

His authoritative tone does nothing to make my tired body get the lead out. This fiasco is situated on a dimly lit shore in Outer Banks, North Carolina at five in the freaking morning, so there will be no pep in my step any time soon. Dude is gonna just have to deal with it. It's what he gets anyway.

"Your name." His deep, raspy voice rings out

over the sleepy morning.

Looking up, I find his vivid blue eyes fixed on me. "Harper Blume," I answer. My defiant chin jerks up like a thug instead of the recluse ghost writer I really am.

"This class begins at five."

"Yep." I place my water bottle down on a picnic table with a bit more force than I should, sending a popping echo to clang out. Choosing to act like I did it on purpose, I jut my chin out a bit further and move to stand beside a thick woman with brown hair at the back of the group.

"It's almost five after." He crosses his intimidating arms. Those babies are roped in taut muscle and defined with a few impressive tattoos.

Well, they should be intimidating, but it's not working on me. This isn't the first round I've had with the jerk. I know this retired Army Ranger's name is Beck McCaffery, and I've paid him a ridiculous chunk of change to take his class. I now also know it's a nonrefundable chunk of change. A fact learned after sobering up the next day and realizing my tipsy-self online shopped for a senseless body boot camp of all things.

Why the drunken idiot couldn't buy a ticket to Hawaii instead of signing up for pure torture is beyond my understanding. It would have cost the same amount!

"What was I thinking?" I mumble under my breath.

Ok, so I know darn well what Miss Tipsy was

thinking. I'm staring at the gorgeous evidence right now and must admit that I'm right ashamed of her shallowness. His black hair is cropped close on the sides while the top is long and unruly. A square jaw sprinkled with just the right amount of stubble, and let's not get started on that masterpiece of a body. This entire debacle put a nonrefundable dent in my checking account all because she couldn't control her inebriated hormones when glimpsing a photo of a shirtless sergeant who was gracing a sponsored post on Facebook.

Only a year ago most links on my newsfeed would try to entice me to try a gazillion calorie dessert recipe or buy women's plus-size fashion that looked nothing like the photos. Now they constantly try luring me to try new fitness crazes. And just how do these suckers know what to tempt me with on my social media? Internet spies, I tell ya! No internet search engine is safe and that's helped me get into hot water this time.

At least the ad wasn't marketing anything false for a change. The photo had captured the soldier from behind—broad shoulders bare except for an impressive tattoo veining out along his right side, tapering into a lean waist with only a pair of fatigue cargo pants hanging dangerously low on his hips— with him peering over his shoulder. Just let me say for the record, never has the definition of a smolder been more clearly represented.

I compare the real-life version to the photo. From the clingy muscle shirt showing off ripped abdominal peaks just under the material to those workout shorts showcasing a toned set of tanned legs, the man defines appealing on a whole new level.

I'm over being ashamed of my tipsy-self and am giving her an attaboy when I notice he's barking something. My eyes zip back to his stern mouth, but have missed the lecture he was divvying out.

"Do you understand?" Plump lips move, flashing a set of pearly white teeth from just behind the snarl.

My gaze peels away from his mouth and roams up to find him looking right at me. *Not good.*

"What?"

The trainer's thick brows pinch as he releases a harsh sigh. "For every minute late after today, the offender will owe me a mile. I won't waste your time and won't put up with you wasting mine."

He begins pacing as I mutter, "Yes, *sir*," but my sarcasm halts his steps.

Shoot.

"Mrs.—"

"Miss," I correct, but don't know why.

"Miss Blume wants class to begin with one hundred jumping jacks. Go!"

The entire class jumps at his order like frightened kittens, but when I hesitate, he wraps his mouth around that whistle and the group instantly freezes at the annoying sound he elicits from it.

"We do this class as one sound unit. Begin again. Together this time. Go!" he yells with those aqua-colored peeps glued to me.

I'm about to throw my hands in the air and fake

the jump when he blows on that darn whistle again. This time the group joins him with glaring in my direction. Perfect. Now I'm gonna be deemed the troublemaker of the class when all I wanted was to be the wallflower.

"Again. Go!"

An hour of agony dredges by with that stupid whistle haunting my every move with its high-pitched squeal. By the end of the session, my spandex shorts designed to hold my body into respectable place feel like they've shrunk two sizes with the addition of a gallon of sweat that seeped into the material. The cooldown and stretches do nothing to alleviate my discomfort. And my lax performance earned me no friends today.

Gathering my empty water bottle, I give it my best effort to not limp away from the beach, but I'm totally failing. My muscles are already having a temper tantrum.

"Blume!"

Oh shoot. A shadow creeps over my shoulder but my legs hurt too bad to make a run for it, so I have no choice but to acknowledge him.

Tightening my wilted excuse for a ponytail, I keep my back to the instructor and mumble, "Yes?" I sweep the long mass of hair over my shoulder, noticing the natural curls have rebelled into frizzy disarray from the sweat and humidity.

"Be on time and leave the attitude home from now on. I won't tolerate it."

Well, I have no choice but to spin around on my

sore heels and face off with this bossy giant, barely containing a wince from the painful action. "Give me my money back like I so kindly asked over the phone last week, and you won't ever have to tolerate me again." We went several phone rounds to no avail.

With his arms crossed, jaw flexing in a menacing tick, it's obvious there will be no give on the subject today either. I'm ready to concede to my monetary loss and limp away for good, but halt when he goes to flapping those annoying lips.

"I already told you, no refunds. I don't go back on my rules, no matter the excuse. And let's be clear here, that's all you got."

"Signing up for this class was a huge mistake." My hands wave around the beach, as though it's to blame.

"Maybe this will teach you a good lesson on making hasty decisions without proper thought first. Won't hurt you to learn what commitment means while you're at it."

"You know nothing about me." The words hiss out of me as my own arms cross, although they aren't anywhere close as notable as his tanned toned ones. "I'll have you know, I've lost close to a hundred pounds over the last few years. I think the lesson on commitment has already been aced."

My words pull no resolve from his stern glare. "Good. You should have no trouble seeing this course to the end." With that, he turns and walks away.

"What? No goodbye? No kiss my—"

"See you Thursday. On time," he calls out over

his broad shoulder without slowing.

That man walks way too gracefully to be that big. I have no choice but to stand here and observe his fluid stride, confused and at awe, until he disappears behind a small patch of trees that conceal the parking lot from the beachfront park.

With no fluid grace to be found on my part, I hobble over to my golf cart to begin the short trek home. This man has ticked me off just enough to see this boot camp torment to the very end.

Even if it kills me…

*****

Feminine elegance is what the white sundress and delicate stiletto sandals would be considered if I wasn't walking around in this outfit as bowlegged as an ancient cowboy who has ridden one too many horses in his day.

Every stilted move my body makes screams a reminder of the morning's torture session. Squats and suicide drills are of the devil! And trying to sit or pee? Forget about it!

For this reason, I have vowed to not take one sip of anything during this book release party. Fear of a potty break ending in a 911 call keeps my thirst in check, even though some liquid courage sure would come in handy right about now.

"Tea?" A cute server presents a tray of mason jars filled with the maple-colored temptation. No doubt the southern nectar is as sweet and syrupy.

Parched. I'm absolutely *parched*. I need the entire tray to quench this thirst.

After trying to swallow the desert residing in my throat, I manage to croak out, "No thank you."

The server offers a polite smile before moving through the crowded yard that's hosting tonight's shindig. He makes a beeline to the guest of honor for the evening and the confident beauty gladly accepts the offered mason jar, raising it slyly toward me in a private salute as she winks one of her golden eyes.

Wishing for my invisibility shield will do me no good tonight. Every part of my dream is front and center to be celebrated with the masses. Even though tonight is honoring my accomplishment—formed from the very words that poured from the recesses of my soul and created another #1 bestseller overnight—Roselyn Scott stands in my rightful spot to take the glory. And I was the idiot to agree to it. She radiates southern elegance in a creamy lace dress with her dark hair swept into a soft updo. No one knows that gorgeous black woman is the beautifully fabricated face for this cowardly white woman's stories. An unlikely team is what we've become, but it somehow works.

A little over seven years ago, I was too shy, too depressed, too uncomfortable with my obesity, too *everything* to be the face behind my novels. When my agent approached me with this idea of ghost writing, it felt like a win-win at the time. I got to express a created world through my words without having to be in the public eye.

"Might I offer you a glass of iced tea, ma'am?" another server asks, nudging my attention away from my musings.

My mouth is pasted shut, so I can only respond by shaking my head. Once I'm alone again, I pop another mint into my mouth and beg it to form some moisture while edging along the group of jovial guests. In the beginning of this well-constructed act, I would have hid in the corner somewhere, but I'm overwhelmed with the need to step out of this sticky shadow that has no desire to release me.

Tired of limping around the pristine yard that is glowing like a field of fireflies from the strands of twinkling lights strung high in the trees, I search out something to lean against and decide the side porch rail will have to do.

"Great location, isn't it?" The familiar huskiness of Maxine's voice reaches me as I head up the stairs, trying not to wince with each step.

"It's quite sophisticated." I glance up at the gracious antebellum home with her wide wraparound porches. She is a grand hostess and her lawn holds several tables with an abundance of southern cuisine.

"So it meets your approval?" Maxine looks at me over the top of her bright-pink glasses. The spectacles cast a violet hue to her gray eyes.

A light breeze carries the savory scents of food to me. Inhaling the aroma deep enough to send a rude growl through my stomach, I scold myself for setting this latest book in the heart of the south. You cannot have a setting deeply rooted in the south without having southern food specialties springing from the branches. That would be like serving tea without the sugar—a cardinal sin in the south.

I gaze longingly at the table serving grits cakes topped with shrimp, mini buttermilk biscuits, and fried chicken drummettes. The table next to it is just as tempting with various mini pies. My mouth waters from just thinking about the chocolate pecan pie. As a recovering food addict, I penned my own personal hell in this thriller and am now snared in the midst of this traditional porch party to celebrate my self-inflicted suffering for at least another hour.

"Well, does it or not?" my feisty agent demands.

A soft laugh draws my attention to the other end of the front porch before I can answer, finding Roselyn clinging to a handsome man while she giggles about who knows what. All eyes are trained on the dark beauty, but as another one of my favorite songs from The Lumineers starts filtering through the outdoor sound system, I'm reminded that the entire night has been catered to my likings. Not hers.

That should make me feel better. *Should* being the operative word. It doesn't.

I glance at my petite literary agent who considers herself my angel, but can be confused as the devil's assistant most of the time.

"You did good, Maxine. This place looks right out of the pages of the book."

"That cover was quite inspiring." She motions to

the six-foot banner on a stand beside an ancient oak tree. A small group of people are gathered, studying the book cover. "We should see about the Thortons doing the next cover as well."

I discovered the image of the aged barn on a magazine cover a few years ago and knew instantly it was the barn in my book where the murderer took his victim. Luck would have it, JP Thorton and his wife Willow were happy to work some editing magic to transform the tranquil night scene into an eerie image full of foreboding, clueing the reader in to the evil lurking just inside the hard cover.

"About the next book, have you considered what we discussed?"

She bites her glossy pink lip, giving me all the answer I need. Rolling my eyes, I start to leave but she reaches out to stop me.

"Lovely, can't we just celebrate you tonight and figure that out after this book tour?"

"Maxine," a deep voice interrupts.

We both follow it to where a distinguished yet a tad bit geeky man is settling onto the top porch step beside the railing I'm stiffly leaning against. The bowtie and the thick pair of glasses sitting askew on his nose scream it. His salt-and-pepper hair and deep laugh lines suggest he's getting close to the fifty-year mark. A silver fox in geek's clothing for sure. He would make one interesting book character. One that seemed harmless, but by the end... BAM! It's discovered the quiet professor is the killer. I blink the scenario away, filing it in the back of my mind to explore later, as Maxine lays her charms on thick.

"Adrian," Maxine coos. "So good to see you." Her grin could be best described as a bit maniacal.

The gentleman doesn't seem to notice her rabid manner. His scrutiny lies on me. "Who is this young lady?"

I offer my hand for him to shake. "I'm Harper—"

"She's Roselyn's assistant," Maxine adds quickly.

"Is that so?" Adrian asks with hints of amusement in his tone.

I narrow my eyes at Maxine and say, "That's what they keep telling me, but I'm not quite sure. How about you? Who do they tell you to be?"

Adrian releases my hand and chuckles. "I'm the president of Wild Idea Publishing House. No one tells me who I have to be but *me*."

A brutal spasm hits my sore abs from the shock of his words. Holy moly, I just sassed *Adrian Wild*, who is sort of my new boss. I can't help but shoot a sidelong glance at Maxine, only to be hit with another spasm in my gut. If her eyes could literally pierce, I would be bleeding out on the floor right this minute. I swear her peeps hold a red tinge to them now. *Get back, demon.*

Roselyn's *actual* assistant rushes over in a tizzy and pulls Maxine away, mumbling something about an emergency, but not before my spunky agent mouths, BEHAVE in my direction.

"Why don't you join me?" Adrian pats the space beside him.

There's no way I can sit or I'll be stuck there the

rest of the night until someone rescues me. Nope. Gonna keep on standing. Playing it off, I pat the top of the railing. "Or you could just mosey over here and join me."

Adrian chuckles again, seemingly amused by everything I do, as he stands and maneuvers to my side. He leans beside me and scans the crowd. "So, tell me what you think about the new book."

My tender shoulder offers a stiff shrug. "It's okay."

"Just okay?" The man is now smirking at me. *Does he know who I really am? No way, could he?*

"What do *you* think about it?" Leaning closer, I whisper, "You can be honest. I won't tell Roselyn."

His gaze shifts from me to Roselyn and then back to me. "Loved it. If Janet Evanovich and James Patterson had a literary love child, this book would be it. All of the books so far would be, if I'm honest."

"Wow. That's quite a compliment." There's no holding my own smile back.

"What I would give for a glimpse inside that creative brain…" Adrian shakes his head and takes a sip of the tea a server just handed him. The condensation on the jar looks good enough to lick.

I look away with hopes of ignoring my overwhelming thirst and begin rambling. "The majority of the reading world loves a good mystery. They love to get lost in the suspense, but not so deep that they can't find their way out of the book. And real life is so stressful nowadays that they're dying for a genuine laugh. My favorite part is that these characters are dynamic and can be complicated, but never take themselves too seriously."

"That's what I like as well." Adrian takes my hand again and leans close. "I'm glad you are on our team, Miss Blume. It's time you stop allowing them to tell you who to be."

Frozen in disbelief, I can do nothing but watch him walk away.

How does he know who I am?

Chapter Two

How does Adrian Wild know who I am?

The frustrating question plagues me all the way home from the book release party. No way would Maxine tell and chance ruining her golden ticket. Someone has ratted me out. I don't know whether to be hurt by someone's disloyalty or to be grateful to them. I'm leaning toward grateful. It's time.

Change… More changes need to be made. Shoot, my cholesterol is in check, my heart isn't swimming in a vat of fat anymore, and my butt fits properly in a single-digit pair of jeans. But is my life really healthier? Jury is still out on that one. The problem is there's a darkness residing in my bones so debilitating that some days I'm unable to make it out of bed. And that shouts at me that more change is needed.

With no answer on how to fix any of that, I brush it to the side and focus on the light shining from my den as I park the car in the driveway. It's a tradition of sorts for the last five years and I'm comforted in it continuing tonight. Knowing he's in my house waiting to celebrate or console or whatever I need from him, causes a stinging in my eyes. I blink several times to rid the emotions begging to bubble out and head inside.

Soft music wafts to the foyer in greeting as I close the front door behind me. Kicking off my shoes, I limp to the den where the devastatingly handsome man sits, one leg resting on the opposite knee and an arm slung in casual grace over the back of the overstuffed sofa.

"Congrats, darlin'." Jack raises the crystal flute in his hand toward me. His voice as smooth and refreshing as the sparkling liquid in that glass promises to be.

"Thanks, Jack."

His dark eyes assess my stilted gait as I step closer. "What's up with that? You look like you got the raw end of the deal against a bull at a rodeo."

"Leave it to you to go vulgar at the first opportunity presented." I snatch the flute out of his hand and down it in one satisfying gulp before handing it back for a refill. The tickling heat spreads down my throat and settles deep inside. "Keep 'em coming. I've gotta catch up." A grunt escapes me as I ease down onto the couch.

"Did you fall flat on your sweet little behind tonight?"

He's still holding the empty glass, so I point to the chilled bottle of champagne on the coffee table. "I went to that stupid body boot camp this morning. Sorry to disappoint, but no embarrassing follies tonight or any bull fights."

"Dang… I was ready for the details." Jack refills the flute and hands it over like the gentleman he was raised to be, but normally doesn't practice.

This time I use a little restraint and only take a generous sip while looking around the cozy beachside cottage that's comfortably dressed in a shabby chic style. Pride places a faint smile on my lips, reminding me how ghost writing hasn't been such a bad end of a stick. Maybe the stay-in-the-shadows plan should continue.

I raise my glass toward the teak bookshelf by the fireplace. It holds the testament of my success, seven NYT bestsellers, before draining the glass. There went my restraint...

"Whoa there, darlin'."

"Don't whoa me. I need some liquid lubrication for my sore joints and bruised ego." I'm cringing before finishing the sentence, knowing he's about to put me in my overindulging place.

A grimace dances along his handsome features as he pushes a hand through his perfectly tousled brown hair. "You know this is a celebratory toast. Be of little wine, young lady."

"Oh, great day, now you're going to go all spiritual on me." I roll my eyes.

"If you're looking for a remedy, I can offer you some TLC." He puckers his lips and leans my way, but I quickly place a hand over his face to shove him away. The sucker licks my palm in retaliation.

"Eww. Gross, Jack! I'd knock you with a pillow if I could lift the dang thing." Another grunt escapes me when I try raising my legs onto the coffee table. My feet remain on the floor, so I give up the notion and slump further into the cushions of the couch.

"I thought you were just going to count that obscene class fee as a loss and move on." He slumps beside me.

"You know how stubborn I am. I figured if the jerk wouldn't reimburse me, he'd at least be stuck dealing with me for the next two months."

Jack's laughter bounces around the room. It's as rich and soothing as the two drinks I've had, but also leaves me wanting more as always.

"At least you're getting out of the house. I'm proud of you."

"You're proud I'm taking a class to be vindictive?" I snort.

"Did you show up and act like a brat?" His perfectly groomed eyebrows hitch up.

I shake my empty glass and he obliges by picking up the bottle. "That was the plan, but Sergeant Jerk didn't give me a chance to misbehave. And now I'm so sore, I was scared to have a drink at the party for fear a potty break would end up in a fire department rescue."

The bottle hovers over my glass as Jack's brows now pinch together. Knowing what's coming, I try snatching it from his grasp, but he's quicker and pulls it just out of reach.

"Do we seriously need to have this talk again?"

"Jack—"

"You're not that overweight woman anymore. And, sweetheart, you've never been rescue squad heavy." He sighs heavily and shakes his head. "I really wish you saw your true self."

"Easier said than done," I whisper, wondering how different my life would have been had he not left me. I brush those sore thoughts away and go for self-demeaning. "My outfits hide a lot of imperfections."

His features transform from concern to raucous challenge instantly. "Take that dress off and let me be the one to decide that." His hand starts to tease the hem of the dress, but I slap it away. "I've seen you naked before. No need in being shy about it now."

"Knock it off. We were all of three years old at the time," I remind him. Jack opens his mouth to obviously deliver something inappropriate, but I quickly add, "Just pour the drink already!"

I'm beyond relieved when he lets the subject go and finally delivers a small refill. Clinking the bottle to my glass, he joins me in a drink. The bubbling liquid leaves a heady warmth in its wake as I snuggle closer to my best friend.

Our history is a simple one. Kids who lived next door to each other and seemed to always end up in the same class throughout elementary school. But that's where the simplicity veered off. We are both from old-money southern families who are blessed in abundant wealth and burdened with scandalous history. The scandals were as old as the money, but the Calloway Family had had enough by the time Jack and I were nine. They left Savannah, Georgia and moved clear across the country to Portland, Oregon the day after Jack's tenth birthday. What a cruel gift that was. Suddenly, my best friend was gone with only loneliness to keep me company in my family's grand Georgian mansion.

Jack filled the holes formed from the neglect of my parents and the isolation that came with my life of privilege. Without him, I became lost for well over a decade.

I lean my head against his shoulder and inhale his subtle cologne. The familiar hints of eucalyptus and mint make me smile. "I missed you."

"Three whole days without me had to be pure misery," he teases, not knowing my thoughts are lingering in the past.

With my best friend gone, food became my go-to to combat the dark solitude surrounding me. Luckily, he found his way back to me after college. Jack was the one to finally talk me off the obesity ledge. One look at the hurt in his eyes when he showed up at the cottage, and I knew the cold hard truth had come home to roost. The pain he reflected was so severe, there was no mistaking him taking the neglect of my body personal. His words that day stung as he held me.

"Darlin', why did you do this to yourself?"

Jack saw me and my self-inflicted wounds for what it was, unlike my parents or the rest of the world. They didn't see me at all. He called me out on it and then remained steadfast with helping me conquer my weight issue. It took a while to get my act together on the weight loss, but I've still not figured out how to get past my low self-esteem.

"I'm so glad tonight is over with," I mumble,

fatigue settling into my bones.

"How did it go?" He takes my glass and places it and the bottle on the table.

I notice he shoves it out of my reach.

"Same as always. Roselyn sparkled. I mostly hid. Maxine tried passing me off as the assistant again." I decide not to tell him about Adrian Wild, thinking I may have made the whole exchange into something it wasn't. It's a weird writer trait I possess—always creating a story out of nothing.

"Did you start speaking in Spanish like last time?"

"No. I went for honesty in a roundabout snarky way."

Jack pats my leg. "That's my girl. Did you tell Maxine the ghost gig is up?"

He's been on me for the last few years to put an end to ghost writing, so I already know he's about to lay into me. I feel it coming and go on the defense. "I tried, but she brushed me off again."

"Because you let her." He turns so I have to pick up my head and meet his eyes. "Seriously, Harper, you've got them all wrapped around your little finger. There's no excuse for you being such a chicken."

"Around my little finger? Hardly."

"Oh? Explain to me this, why would a release party for a mega-successful book be held in a sleepy coastal town instead of New York or California?"

"The inner banks area was the perfect backdrop for the party, so I wanted it to be there," I explain.

"Exactly! *You* wanted it and they made it happen for *you*. You have enough authority to make them be here tonight on your terms. Heck, I bet you even had the final say-so on the details of the party. Think about all of the untapped power you have at your pretty little fingertips."

I nod dismissively. Too tired to go there tonight. "How was the soft opening at Calloway Shores?"

Jack eyes me, clearly trying to decide whether to allow me to change the subject or not. His lips eventually pull into a smirk. "Darlin', there was nothing soft about it. We were hard at it the entire night, or I would have been by your side at that fancy porch party."

Jack's parents made sure to provide their son with an expensive business degree. Jack, in return, took his wealth of knowledge and has opened four of the hottest restaurants along the East Coast with it.

We talk a while longer, but I'm still thirsty, so I produce a yawn and say, "I can barely hold my eyes open."

"Need me to tuck you into bed?"

"No thanks." I yawn again and this has him rising to his feet.

Jack bends down and places a kiss onto my forehead before gathering the champagne flute and bottle. I remain on the couch and mournfully listen on as the remaining contents of the bottle pours down the kitchen sink.

"Good night, darlin'," Jack calls out from the foyer.

"Good night," I reply, infusing as much sleepiness in my tone as possible.

I anxiously wait several minutes past hearing the lock slide into place on the front door and then the sound of his car driving off before I make a move. My body protests, but I manage to make it off the couch and to my bathroom. The white floral arrangement taking up most of the vanity's counter space catches my attention as soon as I flip the light on.

This is another one of Jack's traditions. He's given me flowers for as long as I can remember. The first memory of him doing this was maybe around age five or six. It was only a fistful of wilted dandelions and when I brought them inside and placed them in one of my mother's mini vases, she was appalled.

"Those things are weeds that are fitting for the garbage. Not a crystal vase." She snatched the tiny bouquet out of her precious vase and ordered the maid to dispose of them.

I was heartbroken and ran to my room, but later on the maid snuck in with the dandelions. She had placed them in an old coffee cup. "You know the meaning to a dandelion, child?"

"No ma'am." I wiped the tears away and sat up on the bed.

She sat the cup on my dresser and turned to offer a smile. "They are a gift of happiness and faithfulness."

Both meanings fit Jackson Calloway's friendship like a custom-made suit.

Recalling that fond memory, I smile while testing the buttery soft petal of the white flowers. I lean in and take a testing sniff, finding the flowers to hold an exotic smell that's quite intense. I pluck the card out that's nestled amongst the lilies and read it.

The Casablanca is an oriental lily. It symbolizes success and celebration. Tonight, I celebrate you, darlin'. Love, Jack

Ever since I shared with him what the maid had shared with me, Jack always includes the meaning of the flowers he sends to me. He's my dearest yet only friend, and this double-edged sword of my reality always leaves me in a state of gratefulness with a side of hollowness.

"And now it's my turn to celebrate," I say to no one while limping back to the kitchen where the bottle of bourbon awaits.

The first shot burns considerably and evokes a cough, but by the third it's as smooth as glass. I ease over to the back of the couch and gaze outside at the ocean waves bathed in moonlight. I raise the bottle to the beach before taking a considerable drink.

*****

Everything hurts. Head pounding, legs cramping, back aching, and neck kinking. Every single inch of my body is in agony.

I try adjusting in the bed, but my face comes in contact with something cold and hard. Prying my eyes open and blinking them a few times, I realize my bed is actually my spa tub. And a beach towel is in the place of my fluffy comforter.

While I contemplate on how I ended up here, Jack walks in and casually sits down on the closed toilet seat. I know he knew I'd end up doing this and also knew I'd need him this morning. If everything didn't hurt so badly, I'd be embarrassed.

"What, Jack?" I mutter, but wish I didn't. Two words have the pounding in my temples picking up speed.

"What are you doing in the tub?" His voice is smooth, sounding well-rested—a total contrast to my scratchy rasp.

I try to sit up, but slump back down when my sore body refuses to participate. "Don't know."

Jack moves over to the sink, washes his hands and combs his hair with the locks instantly cooperating. All the while, I'm trapped in the tub and can do nothing but watch him groom himself.

As he straightens the cuffs of his dress shirt, his eyes meet mine in the mirror. "Laying like that can't be good for your body after that class yesterday." He turns around and studies me.

"Ya think? Why'd you let me sleep here?" I croak out, deciding to place the blame on him.

He crosses his arms over his chest, and I try my darnedest to not ogle. Jack is one extremely good-looking man. I'd go as far as calling him pretty. High cheekbones, long eyelashes, pouty lips…

"Darlin', I left you on the couch last night. This is

all on you." He unfolds his arms and offers a hand to help me climb out. "Come on, you lush. Up you go."

As soon as I take it, he pulls me up and all of that bourbon churning in my gut comes up as well. All over his nice shirt.

Talk about a whiskey sour...

Chapter Three

Two weeks of determination have painfully gone by with me resolute on getting my money's worth from Sergeant Beck McCaffery. I've dragged my tired, aching body to the beach at least ten minutes early each Tuesday and Thursday morning to prove to the jerk I know all about commitment. I also express to him that I'm all about making his life equally as hellacious as his class is making mine. Each morning I stand beside the heavy-set woman, who doesn't acknowledge my presence, griping and complaining about each fitness task Beck divvies out.

Perhaps this is why the woman chooses not to speak. I can't even muster up one give-a-care over that at five in the morning. My mind has been trained on the fruitless attempt to garner some control over my life. I wish that was as easy to not care about as it is in not gaining a single friend from this class.

I'm still ticked at Maxine for blowing me off about ending the ghost writing gig. She has only responded via text message since the party, and only sends the record-setting sales numbers as proof I should just shut up and keep doing what I'm told. I'm sick of being told to sit in the corner and be quiet.

These poor souls in body boot camp get to be the

victims of my wrath. I almost feel remorseful until Sergeant Jerk pulls me to the side after each class to deliver an attitude adjustment that I adamantly ignore. I'm diligent on pointing out that all he has to do is hand me my money back and the entire group would be rid of me, but he's as stubborn as I am and won't budge. *Jerk.*

"Today is all about plyometrics." Beck paces in front of the class. A hat is pushed low on his head, concealing those electric-blue eyes. "I want to see space between your feet and the sand today. We're going to begin with a power skip warm-up. Follow me." He takes off down the beach in a *skip*. Seriously.

"Skipping? Are we preschoolers?" I shout from the back of the line.

No one even acknowledges a word I just said, as usual, but it doesn't deter my rant from continuing.

"We pay you hundreds of dollars for this crap?" I grunt and sluggishly skip by myself with the group putting a good bit of distance between us until Beck backtracks and begins skipping beside me.

"Pick up your knees!" He barks the command out, causing my body to automatically rebel against me by obeying him. "Faster! Faster!"

"Stop yelling at me!" I scowl up at him.

"Then do what you should and stop acting like a two-year-old!" His gruff voice shouts each word as he glares down at me from underneath the brim of his hat.

His formidable stature communicates pure intimidation. I should cower. I should pee my pants.

Instead, my stubborn nature takes over the situation. I've wasted too much of my life by cowering down. Still do, but something here says I don't and won't take it quietly from him. Obedience is evidently what he's used to, but sass is what this overgrown jerk is gonna get.

"No!" I slow to a walk. "I'm a grown woman and do as I darn well please."

"A *grown* woman would accept the responsibility of something she's committed to and do it to the best of her ability. She certainly wouldn't be making a fool of herself like you!" He has enough nerve to move behind me and give me a not-so-nice shove. "Get going!"

His comment has the effect of being slapped in the face and has my mouth going mute. Any comeback for his snide remark will only make me sound stupid and immature, so I swallow it back down. I try slowing again after a few stuttered skips, but his large body eliminates almost all of the space between us from him skipping so close. If I do slow, we will both be on the ground.

"Oh, so you're gonna bully me into this today?"

"If that's what it takes. Speed it up!" A heated wall of muscle presses into my upper back as he continues shouting out orders, causing the tension between us to escalate. "Knees up! Faster!"

"You're in my personal space! Back off!"

"Do something about it!" He growls the challenge as his thighs begin meeting the back of my butt.

Him this close to me feels almost intimate and has

me all flustered. Confused by how his touch and heated words affect me, I do something about it. My feet kick into gear and put a safe distance between us. Enough so that I can breathe marginally better.

The demonic skip continues for miles. I swear we've crossed at least one state line before he commands the group to turn around and head back. Once we are in our designated spots, the lady I've attached myself to, whether she likes it or not, is doubled over and vomiting. Beck pays her no attention, just launches us right into burpees and then on to squat jumps. By the end of class, my body is trembling from the exertion and the recurring limp in my walk has returned.

The group staggers off like a bunch of dazed zombies, but I'm unable to even do that. I drop to the sand like a sweaty sack of potatoes and stare blankly at the ocean.

"You're going to be the biggest pain my backside has ever known for the next month, aren't you?" Beck walks over and sits gracefully beside me. The man is too dang agile for such a giant. His height has to be closer to seven foot than six.

"We know how you can remove that pain," I mumble while willing my eyes to lock on the waves. "Just give me my money back and I'll disappear."

"What would be the fun in that?" He chuckles quietly as though he doesn't want to share it with me.

We remain silent for a while, listening to the seagulls squawking at their breakfast along the shore. My eyes grow heavy in contentment.

Too tired to put the effort in to be rude, I decide to try on an air of civility and comment, "I'm surprised by the various dynamics of those attending your class."

"Oh, so you do know how to be pleasant."

I glance over and catch the smirk forming on his lips. And that makes me want to slap it off. "Baby, I know how to do a lot of things and do them well."

That got rid of the smirk, but now those wicked lips are parted in the most welcoming way. The heat climbs my neck and on to my cheeks.

"What else can you do *well*?" His thick eyebrows slowly lift as his raspy voice delivers the dare.

Have I mentioned how incredibly sexy that gruff voice is?

What the heck is wrong with me? I go from civility to sauciness within two sentences. The blame for my verbal nonsense is on the endorphins that are finally kicking in. I can't believe I just sat here beside this handsome jerk and quoted a flipping line from a chapter I wrote last night.

"I don't do a darn thing well. You'll just have to overlook me. I'm sleep deprived." I start to list even more excuses, but clamp my mouth shut when he places his hand on my knee.

"Harp, I've witnessed you doing quite a few things well. You have stubbornness down to an art form. And when you don't think I'm paying attention, you do the exercises like a boss. No more of that self-depreciation. I won't put up with it." He removes his hand, turns his hat backwards and leans back on his elbows, taking on such an appearance of calm it relaxes me. Gone is the gruff intimidation of a drill sergeant, replaced by serenity of a simple man enjoying the sun on his face. Wow.

I look away but can't help but glance back over my shoulder at him. His eyes are shut and his face is tilted toward the sun. It only now registers that he called me something besides Blume. "Harp?"

"Yep. You remind me of a buddy of mine from my unit. Always trying to get under everyone's skin by harping on nonsense and mouthing off all the time. Ironically, his name is Harper and we've always called him Harp. It suits you, too."

"I don't know whether to be offended or flattered."

Beck chuckles a little louder this time, sharing the warmth of it with me and danged if I don't like it.

He keeps his eyes closed, so I take the time to give him a thorough looking over. There's barely any evidence of sweat on his white sleeveless tee, which blows my mind since I could wring my tank top out it's so soaked. He crosses his long legs at the ankle, showing off miles of bronzed skin. A burn scar catches my attention where it peeks out at the edge of his dark gym shorts. It runs along the side of his kneecap and makes me hurt just by looking at it. That deal with a momma kissing her baby's booboo better runs through my mind as I demand my hands to keep to themselves. I glance back at his face and freeze with finding those blue jewels watching me. His bold irises remind me of the turquoise water along the coast of Barbados. Exotic and alluring.

Seems we are heading toward a territory I'm unfamiliar with, making my cheeks heat and my stomach to flutter. It feels like he sees way more than he should. Wanting to get off this uncomfortable track, I veer it back to my comment from earlier. "You should advertise that your class is designed for only diehard fitness buffs and soldiers."

"My courses are structured for all fitness levels."

I cough at that absurdity. "Hardly. I can't even walk off the beach right now. And that poor woman was throwing up between sets."

"Nadine?"

"Is that her name? She won't talk to me."

"Do you blame her? You're trouble." He plows on quickly as soon as my lips part to form a rebuke. "Nadine served two tours in Iraq. She knows what rigorous training is all about. She can handle it, and so can you if you'd stop fighting against everything I tell you to do."

I ignore the last part and ask, "How'd she get so out of shape?" I'd say Nadine is at least two hundred pounds. It's hard to picture her as a fit soldier.

"Like most moms, I suppose. She retired from the military to start a family. Popped out a few babies and got wrapped up in raising them. She forgot to take care of herself, but wants to reclaim her health."

"Like most moms? Not like mine." I shake my head and go back to checking out the ocean. With the day being so early, no one is bothering it yet. It's rather tranquil.

"Your mom is good at balancing kids and herself?" Beck asks, misunderstanding my comment.

"Just one kid and the various nannies got paid to balance me. Made it easy to stay number one on her list." I snort again. "I never was more than an accessory to my parents..." I bring out an exaggerated southern drawl and imitate them.

"'Darlin', does this child go well with my plans for tonight?'

'No, not at all. Put it away.'

'Honey, does this child pair well with my charity event?'

'I do believe so. Bring it along.'"

Shocked by the word vomit that just spewed from my mouth, I shoot to my feet and go to take off to get away from the embarrassment, but my leg chooses to catch a cramp and sends me back to the sand. I cling to it and groan in pain.

"Roll over," Beck says, but he's already flipping me before I can obey. His large hands deftly work along my calf muscle to work the spasm out. He keeps kneading the muscle until it relaxes enough to release the pain.

My eyes roll to the back of my head and the grunting groans turn into mewling moans. This should be awkward, him touching me. Maybe later, once I'm home, I'll feel differently. But this man's touch is stinging and soothing at the same time, and I never want it to stop. Oh, that feels so heavenly...

"Better?" he asks, not even trying to hide the sarcasm in his tone.

"Yes… but my other leg kinda hurts now." I wait for him to yank me up and send me on my way. Instead, another elongated moan slips from my mouth when I feel the strength of his grip on my other calf.

Beck takes his time, but it's still too soon when he removes his touch. "You good?"

"Well, my back is a little tight." I reach around to clutch my lower back.

He lets out a robust laugh. "Maybe you should schedule yourself a massage."

Grunting, I push to my knees and then on to my feet. "The idea of a stranger's hands all over my body doesn't appeal to me."

Those thick brows of his lift again. Yes, I allowed his hands on me and I'm still confused by that one. When I just stand here like a cheeser, his mouth splits into a grin.

Oh my…

Beck McCaffery was handsome before while wearing his menacing scowl. He was striking while his face rose towards the sun just minutes ago. *But that grin…* The man just stole something from me with it, and I'm all tangled up with trying to figure out exactly what that is.

Flustered, I don't wait around to figure it out. Without another word, I start up the beach and over to my golf cart.

"Be sure to hydrate. And stretch good after your shower," he calls out, but I pretend not to hear him. With him talking about showers and stretching, my entire body is in a mad tizzy.

Once the golf cart is parked back home, an itch to write is crawling all over my skin. I know I should go shower first, but all of these odd emotions have been stirred up this morning and has me heading straight to the office. They're a new experience and my need to express them through writing calls so strongly I'm alarmed by it.

Opening one of the stories I've not shared with Maxine, I plow into the next chapter where I've been stumped on how the new couple felt for one another. There was just no capturing their chemistry. The morning has definitely provided abundant inspiration.

Romance has never been my forte, probably from my nonexistent experience with it in my personal life. I've always skated over the relationships of my characters, adding enough sharp wit to pull the reader in, but the flow of crime and mystery has always come easily. Not sure what that says about me as a person...

But today some wall has toppled down and the words are coming faster than I can type them. It's freeing and I'm so consumed with story, I don't notice the day disappearing into night and then continuing on to another morning.

Somewhere near dawn, I pause long enough to shower and catch a few hours' sleep, and then I'm back in front of the computer.

>

His touch confused Margo. That alone should have been enough of a warning to stay away from the dangerous man. Instead, that electric caress acted like a lure and piqued her interest. She wasn't naïve. She knew Chance was enigmatic, powerful, dominant... and would surely break her, but darned if it wasn't tempting.

"The sun is shining and no cloud is in sight! Come out and play!" Jack sings the words from somewhere in the house, breaking the silence that has surrounded me for the last two days.

I ignore his playful tone and keep typing.

Two more sentences have been typed when suddenly my chair is being whisked across the room with my hands still poised in keyboard position.

"Jack!"

"It's Sunday and you are in desperate need of some vitamin D." He pulls me from the chair and forces me out of the office, stopping long enough at the computer to hit save and then the power button. At least my friend is considerate to an extent.

"I'm good," I protest.

"No. You're pasty. Time to crawl out of the cave for a while."

"I've been to the beach twice this week, I'll have you know." I yank my arm out of his grasp.

"Before the poor sun even rose." He pouts his lips out. "That's unholy. Now go put on a bikini to right your sin." He has the audacity to shove me into the bedroom.

I whirl around and pop his bare chest. "Watch it."

Jack ignores me as usual and shoos me toward the closet. "Hurry up. I'm gonna go drag a few chairs down to the water." He struts out of the room.

Once he shuts the door, I take a step inside the closet, figuring I might as well unearth a swimsuit and keep allowing the world to boss me around for another day.

Ten minutes later, I stomp outside and am instantly blinded by the brilliance of the sun. My hand shoots up to shield my eyes. *Bright light! Bright light!* My inner Gizmo squeals. It's a Gremlins reference. Look it up.

After allowing my sensitive eyes to adjust, I find Jack lounging by the shore with his arms above his head. He looks to be posing for a tanning ad. No doubt, he's intriguing enough it would sell the concept to even a vampire. I plop in the chair beside him and kick my feet up.

He cracks one eye open. "Nice skirt... if you're playing tennis. That suit doesn't right your iniquity."

"What's with you and all of the spiritual references this morning?"

Jack hands me a bottle of high-powered sunblock with a hint of bronzer, knowing my pale skin will burn to a crisp without it. "First off, morning has been gone for a few hours now. Secondly, my parents are visiting and requested I attend church this morning with them. Thirdly, you need to explain the granny suit."

We were both raised in church on an extreme level. It was written in sacred stone to be at church every time the doors were open. People would slide on their holy masks before entering and quickly slipped them back off after shaking the pastor's hand at the end of service. They also had a ridiculous set of rules they expected everyone to adhere to—no dancing, no drinking, no cursing—funny how I've never been able to find those holy no-no's in my Bible, but whatever. The fakeness and man-made rules held no appeal, so we both veered away from church after moving out of our parents' homes.

"Harper." Jack snaps his fingers close to my ear, pulling me from my thoughts.

"What?"

He flicks the hem of the bathing suit skirt. "Answer for your sin."

I smooth the black ruffle back down. It's not as bad as he's making it out to be. The tankini has a halter-top and shows a respectable amount of cleavage. "Thunder-thighs need coverage."

Jack scoffs. "I won't even dignify that idiotic notion with a response."

"Whatever."

"Last word."

"No."

"Yes."

"Whatever."

Instead of continuing our childish banter, Jack huffs and closes his eyes. I grin in victory as I pop open the bottle, bring it to my nose, and inhale the coconut scent it releases.

"Weirdo."

"Call me what you will." I coat my skin with the tropical smelling lotion, loving how it mingles with the briny air to produce the trademark perfume of summer.

"I take it from the typing frenzy I just witnessed, Maxine has you on a tight deadline."

"No. That's one of my other books." I toss the bottle into the caddy on the back of the lounge chair and try to relax.

"Do I get to read it?"

"You always get the first read." Even before Jack moved here, I would send him the first draft. He's brilliant at seeing where a story has an overlooked hole and is quick to explain how to fill it.

"So that makes five stories total you now have hiding on your computer. Darlin', you need to man up and publish them."

"Maybe this skirt is hiding my manliness," I sass back, deflecting the argument that has become a constant between us lately.

His hand darts over and flips the ruffle up to expose the bottoms underneath before I can stop him. "Nope." He mutters something inappropriate under his breath.

"Jackson Calloway! Your foul mouth needs to head back to church." I shove his lingering hand away and glance around at the crowded beach, hoping no one overheard this ridiculous conversation. "Behave or I'm going back inside and securing the deadbolt."

"Yes, ma'am. Please forgive me," he drawls out, his tone dripping saccharine.

We both settle down for a while and just enjoy the sun warming our skin with the breeze keeping it in check. Eventually, it lulls me into a lazy doze.

"Now that is what you call physique art." Jack mumbles.

My eyes open and begin combing the beach for the art. "Who? Where?" I am a people-watching-holic. Weird how a recluse can be addicted to people of all things, but mainly from afar. I blame it on the writer in me, always doing character studies.

Jack points toward the water. "On the surfboard. The one on the right."

It's easy to tell which surfer he's referring to. Even from a distance, the man has a striking body—broad shoulders tapering into lean hips, long legs gracefully braced on top of the board. We watch as the surfer maneuvers a wave in such a fluid motion it's like watching art in motion. Another surfer riding a close wave staggers off his board as it peters out. But not surfer art. Nope, he executes a perfect backflip before disappearing into the ocean, totally owning the water and the board.

"Dang." Jack glances at me briefly before going back to checking out the show. "I need to know what this guy did to get that body and start doing it myself." His head angles to the right and then to the left while flexing his biceps.

I snort then move the sound to a lengthy snicker

when Jack tightens his abs. "You are so vain."

"You still love me." He abandons his peacocking and reaches over to tickle me.

Howling in laughter, I push his hands away. "Knock it off!"

We calm down and return our undivided attention to the artwork owning that surfboard. This time, when the wave dies down, the surfer simply takes a languid step off the end of the board, tucks it underneath his arm, and begins walking toward the shore. As he draws closer, my lungs hold the air in them captive, causing me to gasp for more.

"What's wrong?" Jack asks.

"That's… Give me your towel!" I grab it off the back of his chair before Jack can move and use it to shield my body.

"You know that guy?"

"Yup." My body scoots farther down in the chair, wishing the darn thing would swallow me up. "He's the boot camp instructor from *hades*."

"No way." Jack gasps. "This is *awesome*."

Oh brother. This man loves humiliating entertainment at my expense. "Please don't, Jack." I peek from the edge of the towel and catch sight of Beck walking just to the left of us. He sweeps his fingers through his wet hair, pushing it away from his forehead.

"Hey, man. That was some impressive surfing," Jack calls out to get Beck's attention.

"I'm gonna kill you in your sleep," I growl under my breath.

Jack ignores the comment and lifts his hand to wave, making sure Beck notices us. I look back over and sure enough the man has deviated from walking away to walking toward us. He stops close to the end of my lounge chair. A few drips of ocean have left him and reach my toes where they are sticking out at the end of my shield.

"Nice towel, Harp," Beck comments before looking over at Jack and giving him a nonchalant chin jerk. "Thanks man."

"You didn't perfect those skills with East Coast waves." Jack's tone deepens, as it always does when another man is around. *Men…*

"My old man was a Naval Commander. One perk was him being stationed at some really sweet spots around the world. We spent most of my teenage years in Hawaii," Beck answers, intriguing me.

"Please excuse my girl's rudeness. I'm Jack." He sits up and offers Beck his hand.

"Nice to meet you." Beck takes it, but moves his focus back to me. I can do nothing but stare back like a mute fool.

"Man, you have got to tell me how I can obtain that sharp V." Jack boldly points to where Beck's board shorts are riding low. The deep grooves beginning at his hips and veering south are remarkably defined.

"Lots of lower oblique exercises." Beck answers like that's the simplest thing.

"Maybe I should sign up for body boot camp. Harper, are you hiding a V underneath that top?"

Jack reaches under the side of the towel and, much to my horror, tries lifting the bottom of my top.

"Err!" I try forming his name, but my frozen lips only produce a growl as I give his hand a good whack while pulling the towel back into place. I'm pretty certain my best friend's death is going to be on my hands.

Beck wastes no time moving on after Jack fires off several more workout questions, seemingly not wanting to be bothered on his day off. Thank goodness, because I'm sweltering underneath this towel. Once he's out of sight I push it down to my lap and can finally breathe again.

Jack releases an exaggerated snort.

My temper flares and thaws my frozen tongue. "So glad you're amused."

"Beyond," he bellows out around a raucous laugh. "A guy hits on you and you act like one of those fainting goats that go all stiff and keel over at any sudden attention." Jack stiffens out his legs, rolls to his side, and pretends to faint.

I reach over and slap him hard enough to leave a handprint on his back. I won't kill him today, but I hope to leave a few bruises. The slap resurrects my dead friend, making him roll back over to face me.

"Beck wasn't hitting on me. That was him trying to get under my skin."

"Oh, I bet he'd like to be all about your skin."

"Enough, Jackson!" The man thinks he's a comedian.

Still snickering at his own lame joke, Jackson rolls

to his stomach. "Grease me up, baby."

"I ort not to with you making fun of me." I carefully word it so no lame remarks can be pulled from it. I grab the bottle of sunblock and squirt out a generous glob between his shoulder blades. As soon as my hands touch his olive-toned skin he lets out a suggestive moan.

"Yeah, *baby*…" Moan. "Just like that. Oh *yeah*."

"Stop that!" I slap his firm butt cheek, stinging my hand while glancing around and finding several eyes zeroed in on the Jackson Show.

"Yes! Spank me! I've been a very bad boy!" He yells out, sounding like a sleazy performer.

"You're impossible. I should have stayed in my office." Shaking my head, I leave thick white streaks of the sunblock on his back. No way am I touching him again on this beach. Humiliated, I settle back down in my chair. I'm dying to make a run for it, but surely everyone has their focus trained on these two lounge chairs after Jack's little performance. The man should have been an actor.

"Come on, you know you love me."

When I give him no more attention—he's like a child with needing that so much—Jack goes back to sunbathing.

We grow quiet for a while with me not wanting to add any more fuel to Jack's mouthy fire and him texting away on his phone. It's practically attached to him. I don't even know where my phone is at the moment and really don't care.

I'm close to dozing back off when Jack starts

squirming in the chair and grumbling under his breath. A few moments later, he sucks in a long inhale and steals the towel back. Standing up, Jack wraps it around his waist and starts off in the direction of my cottage. "That heavy brunch is hitting my gut hard. I better get to the bathroom before I embarrass myself on this beach."

There's no holding back the unladylike snort as I stand to follow. "*Before* you embarrass yourself? You can consider that deed already done."

He ignores me and doesn't slow until he's disappeared inside the house.

I don't notice Beck sitting on his surfboard until it's too late to act like I didn't. *Shoot.* Jack has left me with no shield, so here I stand all exposed. That tongue of mine refreezes, but I acknowledge him with a forced smile before turning back toward the lounge chairs. Bracing my hands around the top edge of one, I begin a slow progress of lugging it back to the deck. I only make a few steps backwards when suddenly a giant hand reaches close to mine.

"Let me help you," Beck says as he easily clutches one bulky chair in each fist and heads to the deck. He makes it look as effortless as carrying a sack of groceries. "You want them on the deck of that house Jack just went into?"

"Umm… Yes. That's my house," I stutter.

Stunned, I slowly follow behind him. Beck is one intimidating man, so normally I'm capable of handling only short spells of looking at him. Right now, I simply cannot look away. My focus is glued on an oak tree with an intricate root system that is growing along the bulging backside of his left bicep. I'm close enough to reach out and trace the black ink, but demand my hands to keep to themselves. And then there is a stunning abstract phoenix rising from vivid flames on his right shoulder. These aren't just tattoos, but works of art that seem to hold a story within them. Oh, how I want them to whisper their secrets…

I nearly head-butt the phoenix when Beck suddenly stops.

He glances over his shoulder. "Where do you want them?"

"Over by the small table is fine." I point to the right of the deck. "I'm surprised Jack took the time to lug those heavy things to the water."

Beck puts them in place and heads back down the steps to where I'm standing. "Your boyfriend is a riot." He shakes his head and gives me a wry smile.

Great. So he definitely just witnessed the ridiculous scene by the water.

"Jack is something else, but he's not my boyfriend." I cross my arms, but realize the action has pushed more cleavage to be on display, so I let them drop awkwardly to my side.

"Does he know that?" Beck eyes me with a good measure of interest.

"Yes, and he also knows I'm currently planning his murder." I look at the set of French doors that lead inside.

"Now you're worrying me."

My focus skips back to Beck. "Why's that?"

He nods his head in the direction to where his surfboard is sitting in the sand, and for some reason I follow him like a well-trained puppy. He sits down, but I remain standing.

"At the end of class the other day you told me you were planning my murder. Just how many murders are you planning?" His eyebrows pull together with scrutiny, but there's tease lilting his question.

My fingers exaggerate a count, thinking Maxine's name should be top of the list. That hussy won't return my phone calls. "Only three." I shrug as if it's no big deal.

"Who's the third?"

My shoulder shrugs again. "No one you know." I slide my right foot in the warm sand, drawing circles. "So... You're an army sergeant/demonic fitness trainer/surfer?"

He laughs, deep and raspy. And that rugged sounds flows over me like warm melted butter. Something is wrong with me—my heart is skipping around, my palms are growing clammy, my eye sight blurs slightly. I should be panicked, but for some reason I find pleasure from the newness of my body reacting in such a wild way.

"Ex-sergeant. I retired after four tours. Well, semiretired is a better description. I still help out with boot camp training and some special assignments. Now I'm pretty much just a *demonic* trainer who grew up on a surfboard." His lips curl on one side.

I do a quick math and guess his age to be somewhere around mid to late thirties. He looks younger though.

"These waves must bore you." My thumb hitches over my shoulder toward the docile water.

He glances at the ocean. "I make do with them."

My curious writer sensors go off and deliver hundreds of questions I want this man to answer. "Why settle here?"

Beck brings his attention back to me. "I still help out with basic training at some of the southeast bases. It's more convenient."

The wind whips my hair across my face. I tuck the wayward strands behind my ear and ask, "You been here very long?"

"Just a few months." Beck reclines onto his elbows and continues to look up at me. This reveals another tattoo etched along his right inner arm. It has a military theme, but I don't want to get caught staring, so I quickly look away.

"Oh."

"How about you?"

Oh no. Now he's becoming inquisitive, too. I'm never comfortable being on this side of it. I fidget, readjusting my weight from one leg to the other and play with the ruffle resting against my thigh. "About ten years."

"Humph. I only live a few houses up that way." He points toward the right of my house. "I'm surprised I've not run into you or your boyfriend before now."

"I don't venture out often, and I believe I already told you Jack isn't my boyfriend. We grew up together."

"Oh, so you decided on a whim to venture out just to make my Tuesdays and Thursdays a living nightmare?" There's no bite to his comment, only tease for some reason.

"Yep. You're such a lucky man," I sass back. "Look, I better go make sure Jack isn't defiling my sacred throne," I say, knowing that made no sense to Beck, but Jack will totally love it.

"So… Is Jack gay?" Beck's voice drops in volume.

"Why? Are you interested?" I can't help but ask.

"In him?" Beck shakes his head slowly. "No. Just trying to make sense of why he wouldn't be playing for more than friendship with such a beautiful spitfire."

His words have me completely flustered. *Flight or fight?* Like the coward I am, it's definitely flight! I turn tail and make a break for it. "Because I'm mean," I blurt out like an idiot before getting out of his earshot.

I'm mean? Really? I'm such a doofus.

"Harper…" Beck calls out, but I keep with the hard-of-hearing act and continue trucking it.

Once inside, I hurry over to the closed bathroom door and pound on it. "You better not be defiling my sacred throne on the Sabbath!"

From the other side, Jack's hardy chuckle echoes like I knew it would.

We both laugh at our lameness. I leave him to take care of his business and pad back to the French doors. As soon as I peep out, my eyes land on Beck. He's right where I left him, but is now stretched out on top of the surfboard looking like he's floating on the sand.

A hand clamps my shoulder, sending me at least a foot off the floor. Pushing a palm against my fluttering chest, I whirl around. "Don't creep up on me like that!"

Jack raises both hands in fake defense. "What's so interesting outside?"

I try moving away from the door, but Jack blocks me in and peers outside. "Jack—"

"Nice view you got there, *Harp*. What's up with that, anyway?"

Wanting to dodge the conversation altogether, I duck under his outstretched arm and head into the kitchen for a glass of water. "He says I remind him of his aggravating buddy named Harper."

"Aww. Ain't that cute."

"Shut up."

Jack meanders around the kitchen island and studies the clock on the microwave. "We need to get ready."

I finish my sip of water and ask, "For what?"

"We have dinner reservations with my parents." He swipes my glass and downs the rest.

"Not me."

"Come on. They want to see you." Jack puts the glass in the half-filled dishwasher before leaning a hip against the counter.

"Nu-uh. Last time was horrid. Your mother

scrutinized every blame bite I put in my mouth like she was waiting for me to flip out and start inhaling everything in sight."

Diane Calloway has never hidden the fact that she's not fond of me. The first time she and Jack's dad, Jackson Senior, visited Jack after he moved here they saw me at my heaviest. I think Diane will always view me as the two-hundred-thirty-pound girl from that day. She looked at me with pure revulsion, and belittled me for ordering a potato to go with my steak that night at the restaurant.

"I'm sorry she makes you feel less than you are, darlin'." Jack drapes his arm around my shoulder and pulls me in for a side-hug. "How about we blow them off and go somewhere else?"

"No. You should spend some time with your parents while they're here." I see the hesitation in his dark eyes, so I add, "Besides, I have reached my limit of public time with you for the day. Your naughty mischief has exhausted me."

He presses his lips into a thin line, not buying my excuse for one minute, but with a long sigh, he lets it go.

Jack heads out shortly after this and I take the time to shower before going back to my office. It's the only place I truly feel that I belong.

In my cave, alone.

Chapter Four

Monday morning, the darkness shows up and starts veining throughout my body. All because of a spiteful email reminding me of my place. The cursor blinks in the reply box while my fingers tap a severe beat against the edge of the keyboard, contemplating a response. The only thing that comes to mind begins with an uncivilized word and ends with *you*. I refrain from sending that and reread the email for the fifth time.

Miss Blume,

Attached is a copy of your contract with Welsh Agency. It states that you are only allowed to ghost write the Breakers Series for Roselyn Scott. Ms. Welsh also wanted you to be reminded of the fact that you are being compensated substantially for your writing, and she feels it is most disrespectful for you to become greedy at this point.

Sincerely,

Kate Singleton, Associate Agent

I wasn't even worth the effort for Maxine to email me personally. That really stings. After staring at the cursor for a few more minutes, I finally form a response.

Ms. Singleton,

Money has nothing to do with my wish to write under my own name. It has everything to do with me needing to get out of this debilitating shadow, so I can have the independence to express myself freely.

Since Maxine is unable to communicate with me properly, I feel it is time for my lawyer to speak for me. She will be hearing from him soon.

H.B.

Now I just need to get a lawyer, a male one at that. Wishing I had someone to talk to sends an ache to set in deep inside me. Jack is the only one I ever discuss this stuff with and he's out of town. My parents would just tell me to be grateful for what I have and that's not what I want to hear. Shoot, they don't even know I ghost write.

I'd say a girls' night would be a great way to get my mind off this mess, but one would have to have girlfriends to pull that off.

Bone-tired, I slump in my desk chair and let the heaviness do its damage. Darkness muddles my vision while the same mantra repeats in my head.

You're not good enough.

No one cares.

No one sees you.

Your life does not matter.

You're all alone.

This is what you deserve.

I'm stuck in this melancholy funk, not able to

move from the office for several hours, until an anxious rage singes it away. I abandon the pity party and go straight into a ticked-off frenzy. With the anger clawing at me from the inside, I pop my earbuds in and crank the iPod up to the highest volume setting and attempt to working it out of my system. I need to drown out the disappointing reality I'm stuck living.

By midnight, my house has been cleaned from one end to the other. The sterile smell of bleach has attached to my skin and clothes. Between the chemicals and the loud music, my temples have begun to drum in a dull tempo. The anger has been worked out of my system, but is now replaced by a fatigued depression. No matter how hard I run from it, that monster always catches up to me.

Shuffling from the laundry room to the den, switching off every light along the way, I go to my hiding spot behind the couch. If my body scrunches close to the corner, I only get a glimpse of the ocean from the French doors. This spot between the couch and wall forms a little alcove of sorts and always gives me the false sense of being hidden from the world. Usually a bottle of bourbon is the only companion invited to this hiding spot, but tonight I settle against the back of the couch and only permit tears to join me. They fall until the dull throb in my temples transforms into an entire percussion section.

After downing a few migraine-strength pills, I move to the bedroom and curl in a ball underneath the blankets of my bed until the alarm clock announces Tuesday-too-darn-early-morning. My first reaction is to throw it across the room and keep on sleeping, but then a set of sparkling blue eyes flash from my memory. I shouldn't want to see Beck, but at the moment, he's the only thing interesting in my life. And that's completely pathetic due to him being my fitness instructor whom I hardly know anything about. But danged if he ain't purty to look at.

A quick shower and a fresh set of workout clothes make me feel closer to human, but one glimpse in the mirror cancels that notion out. Big, poufy pillows sit below my red-rimmed eyes. A futile attempt with an icepack to reduce the swelling has me pushing close to five. Giving up, I throw on a hat to conceal last night's crying spell and rush out the door. It's the first morning I've been late since the first class. Hopefully Beck's threat was all growl with no bite.

By the time I scurry up to the group they are already in the midst of jumping jacks. Angling slightly behind Nadine, I seal my snarky lips and do every exercise Beck divvies out this morning. A whiny comment wants to slip out a few times, but I refrain for fear that drawing any attention my way will result in consequences.

Beck finishes the torture session with four sets of push-ups, adding up to a total of one hundred. My chest burns and my arms tremble, but I hold in the groans.

"That's it for the day. See you Thursday." His gruff voice rings out, followed by several sighs of relief from the group.

Before the group has a chance to scatter too much, I dodge around them for cover with hopes of making it to the golf cart before Beck can make good on his no-late-to-class policy. The mini rescue wagon is in my sight and I'm about to take off like shot when a hand comes out of nowhere and grips my shoulder, sufficiently halting my escape.

"You owe me five miles."

I spin around to dodge his hold on me and sass out, "I owe you nothing."

Those penetrating eyes narrow as he points toward the shore. "To the pier and back is four and a half miles. We'll call that close enough. Now get on with it." He growls the command. It's so full of menacing authority, my legs begin trudging the shore at once.

My body is sending me death threats as I beg it to pick up the pace to at least a sluggish jog. The sand taunts me as it grasps ahold of my sneakers each time one plops down.

"Speed it up!" Beck yells out.

I glance over as he sidles up to me, discovering he's lost his shirt and nearly trip over my own feet. Oh yes. This is the distraction I need from my crappy life. "Stop yelling at me! I can hear you just fine!"

"That's debatable."

"Why are you running?" I huff out, still wobbling around.

He reaches over to steady me, which only makes me stumble more. "For the fun of it," he answers.

"You're a sick, sick man."

Beck doesn't respond, just sets the pace a little faster. My lungs begin to burn and my legs scream at the sand to leave us the heck alone. I have deduced one thing in these five minutes of running and that is only insane people would willingly run on the beach.

I'm. In. Purgatory!

Inhaling enough air to be able to form words, I sputter out, "I'm dying."

"Nonsense. Suck it up."

Unable to form any more words, I growl instead. Real mean-like, too, and that jerk has the audacity to laugh.

"Tell me, Harper. What is it you do for a living?" he asks out of the blue, distracting me from the idea of biting the laugh out of him.

"Grr!" I growl again, but decide to answer a few seconds later with a half-truth. "Freelance writer."

"Yeah? And what does that entail?"

Our feet slap against the shore in a rhythmic thud. I listen to the beat of it for a second to form an answer. "Someone offers me a writing assignment and I write it." There, that should shut him down. Making the mistake of looking over at him, my throat thickens at the sight of all that glistening skin...

"Blume!" His harsh tone pulls my eyes up to meet his.

"What?" I grouch out, ticked he just caught me ogling him.

"I asked you a question." His hard trainer façade has slipped down enough to reveal the smug jerk underneath.

"What?" I grouch out again, not liking that perceptive look on his face. He sees too much.

"Have you written anything I may have read?"

Wiping the sweat from my forehead before it has the chance to sting my eyes, I shake my head. "Probably not. You look like a history buff kind of guy who wants to read about war." Yes, that's too assuming, but I want to shut his questioning down.

"I've lived war firsthand, sweetheart. No need in reading about it."

I squint against the early morning sun, wishing the pier would get off its lazy haunches and meet me at least halfway. "You wouldn't read anything I write."

"I'm pretty versatile. Try me." His dark brows kick up in challenge.

I look ahead, but then back to him, taking a moment to appreciate the appealing contrast of the bright blue of his eyes to the darkness of his eyebrows. Beck is all raw masculinity, no doubt about it.

"Come on, Harper. Tell me." The man isn't even winded. He speaks with such evenness you'd think he's taking a leisurely stroll.

That won't do.

"Steamy romances?" I question.

This only earns a slight curl of his wide lips. "I don't knock anything until I've tried it at least once."

Dang. This makes *my* breathing sputter out. "You've read steamy romance?"

"No, but I wouldn't dismiss the idea of giving it a

go." Sounds like the same answer he just gave me until he adds, "Especially if you're the one penning it."

All I can do is gasp at that, thinking this beach is about to become my burial ground. Eventually, I say, "Too bad. I don't write that stuff."

"Oh. You're not daring enough?" A challenge gleams in his turquoise eyes.

"I'm *versatile* enough to write whatever I so please, but that genre has never appealed to me."

Beck produces a knowing smirk. I'm just not sure what he thinks he knows.

After we finally reach the pier and swiftly turn our backs to it, my breathing relaxes a bit with finally pushing past that runner's wall. It always shows up around mile two.

"Tell me a steamy story, Miss Versatile."

His request slams into me and wrecks my steady breathing.

"What?" I sputter out.

He huffs with a good bit of agitation. "If you say that word one more time, I'm adding a mile." He gives me a pointed look, all business again. "Now show me how versatile your writing craft can be and spin me a love story."

Heat rolls up my neck at the absurdity of this conversation in the midst of a forced run. My resolve shows up and demands I not allow this jerk to get the best of me, because clearly that's his game. No way am I telling him such a story on the fly. In my sleep-deprived state, I'd most likely blurt out one of my daydreams about a hot soldier with aqua eyes.

"How about I describe a physical experience?"

"Whaddaya have in mind?"

Thinking it through for a few minutes, I recall something I read once about pain and pleasure being similar in more ways than not.

"You can't do it?" Beck challenges when I remain mute.

Taking a slow breath, I begin, "A throb dances along in an aggressive beat, burning through my veins. A pressure builds, igniting a fire so intense my body weeps for its release. If the crescendo doesn't hit soon, surely I will perish from the excruciating torment. Every nerve ending spasms, sending sparks to ricochet along my body." Pausing, I hiss a heavy breath out as my hands rub along the curve of my neck. "A fever-pitch ringing strokes my eardrums from the pressure building. It's too much. All too much." I roll my neck and let out a slow moan, while stealing a glance at Beck.

"Whoa now. I think that's enough." He stifles a groan and tries covering it with a cough.

"What? I was just describing the massive headache I had last night. FYI, that's why I was late for class."

The mortification fades from his heated eyes before he rolls them. "Smart-aleck."

My hands shoot up. "I can't help where your dirty mind went." It's all I can do to hold back the giggle begging to be freed. It feels pretty good to get Mr. Alpha Cool flustered. It's what he deserves for making me run almost five freaking miles.

"I think I need to head to church and repent," he muses while slowing his pace.

I'm all grateful to slow right down with him. "Oh, so you're one of those holy rollers? The way you bark at me, I'm surprised. And asking for a steamy story... Shame, shame, shame..." I tsk with a reproachful head shake.

"Maybe *steamy* was the wrong word to use. I meant a girlie romance, but anyway..." He scratches the scruff on his cheek and shakes his head as though to rid himself of the story before turning serious. "No holy roller here, Harp. Just a sinner saved by grace."

"Now that right there sounded much like a holy roller answer." I point at him. "What's the repentance for lust? Don't you have to cut something off—"

"Harp! You just don't know how to let something rest, do you?"

"You do call me *Harp* for a reason." I'm right proud of myself for getting underneath his skin with my flippant remark. That feeling lasts all of two seconds until he speaks again.

Beck halts suddenly and grabs my arm to plant me in front of him. "We're none perfect. I don't claim to be. Some religious groups have put my God in a shiny glass cage, but they're wrong. And closedminded folks such as yourself are being cheated out of knowing a powerful Savior because of it. It isn't worth being flippant over and going to hell. Let's be clear on one thing, heaven and hell are just as real as the air you're breathing and the sweat dripping from your skin." His fingertips glide through the damp trickles along my neck.

I take a step back to put some distance between his touch and his words, confused by how both make me feel. Beck drops his hand and just stares. We say nothing for a strained pause until he turns and begins walking away.

He calls out in a thick voice over his shoulder, "Thursday! Don't be late!"

Some seagulls begin squawking, snapping me out of my daze, so I shuffle over and hop onto the golf cart. I thought I had finally one-upped the sucker with the misleading headache story, but now I realize all the points go to him today. Beck effectively distracted me from the pain of the five-mile run with flirting of all things and also helped block out the pain I've been drowning in lately. Then he rounded it all out by going religious on me. Don't know why, but my insides stir until the pout drops from my lips as they begin to tremble.

The tears flow all the way home as the cart zips down the deserted beach and don't cease until I'm locked away in my office. I take the wild feelings Beck has summoned, mix them with my longing to be free of my dark vices, and allow them to pour out in several chapters.

⁂ ✳ ✳ ✳ ✳

"It's Margo." With a sick stomach, Ward identified the

body, knowing Chance Marx had something to do with this dynamic woman's death. He knew not to trust him. Margo knew not to trust him. But both failed to pay attention to the warning bells, and now Margo had paid for their naivety with her life. One thing in that moment was for certain, Ward wouldn't rest until Chance paid for what he had done.

My aching fingers fly over the keyboard before hitting save. One glance at the wall clock says *you better keep on keeping on*, so I power down the computer. I've really got to stop pulling these all-nighters, especially two in a row. The sleep deprivation is starting to catch up with me in the forms of lethargy and body pain. I caught myself putting the jug of milk in the dishwasher and my dirty plate in the fridge last night and at this moment my entire body feels bruised. Standing, my arms reach over my head with hopes of alleviating the soreness along my spine. When the ache won't relent, I head to the bathroom for a scorching shower.

Once I'm out and redressed in a tank top and spandex capris, I still have an hour before class. There are dishes to be washed, a neglected basket of laundry waiting by the washer, and two toilets needing a scrubbing. That could kill the extra time and keep me awake. Instead, I've got my trusty golf cart scooting along the dark beach, knowing he's already out here setting up.

The beams of the cart's lights catch Beck bent over a giant wagon with massive wheels. My foot eases off the gas pedal to prolong the view. He peeps over his shoulder before standing, both fists pulling a thick rope out of the wagon and into a long straight line. I park and walk back to his wagon and try yanking out a fat kettlebell weight, but give up rather quickly.

"You're incredibly early." He sounds amused. It's way too early in the morning for amusement.

"Not gone to bed yet," I reply, my voice sounding rusty and feeling scratchy from not speaking since Tuesday. A smaller kettlebell catches my attention, so I pull it out and test its weight with a few bicep curls before handing it over to him.

"You've been up all night?" The nightlight from above catches the skepticism skirting his features.

"Yeah. Been on a writing spree. Just wrapped up the climax of the story," I mutter while poking around in his wagon. A stack of orange cones sits in the corner, reminding me of the suicides he made us perform a few weeks ago. I take a towel and stealthy place it over the cones.

"Aren't you tired?" He keeps his focus on me as he fishes the stack of cones out from under the towel.

Guess I wasn't as smooth with the sneakiness as I thought. Dang it.

My tender shoulders shrug as I watch him set the cones in a familiar staggered line. "Yeah, but I knew if I got still I'd never make it to class, so you get an assistant this morning."

Beck nudges me out of the way and lifts three of the kettlebells in one hand, making it quite evident he is in need of no assistance.

"Lucky me," he says, but doesn't come off sullen.

The amusement is still weaving through his tone. It's almost enough to make me grouchy. Who in the heck is chipper at four in the morning?

I motion over the obstacle course. "No plyotheatrics today?"

"Plyometrics," he corrects.

"I know the right term." My heavy eyes roll.

He chuckles at my poor joke. "Today is circuit training. It's good to change up your routine. Muscles memorize a routine and tend to get lazy."

I prop against the giant wagon and regard him. Beck's moves are graceful and determined as always and I'm becoming addicted to simply watching his body move. "Did you go to school for this?" I point to the equipment littering the sand.

"Didn't need school for this. I lived it out in the military, and then taught it out during my last tour as Master Drill Sergeant."

"Wow. Drill sergeant... Now that is *hawt*," I mumble, angling my head to get a better view of his backside as he straightens a set of weights. The sun needs to wake up so I can see better.

He stands back up, looking a bit stunned. "You just call me *hot*?"

My eyes blink, coming close to not reopening. "Oh yeah. Between this sculpted body you've got going on, that chiseled jawline that always has just enough shadow to make any woman's fingertips long to test the texture of the stubble, and the alpha military male persona you'd be one mighty fine study for the hero role in a romance novel." I stop rambling when I notice he's gone still as a statue. "What?"

"You're flirting with me at..." Beck studies the heavy-duty watch on his wrist, "...four fifteen in the morning."

This wakes me up. "I... No... I didn't mean to—"

"Yes, you were." His lips twitch. I'd say he was just poking fun at me, but I don't know him well enough to make that call for sure.

"My mind is still in writing mode. I was pointing out your book character qualities." My hands shoot up in defense. I notice a stability ball resting in the sand and point at it. "I think I need to sit on you... I mean on the ball!" *Did I really just say that?*

I shuffle over to the ball and have a seat before I say something else to embarrass myself. Clearly, the sleep deprivation has wreaked havoc on my brain-to-mouth stop sign. My tired body tries to balance on the wiggly ball, but loses the battle when Beck walks over and leans over me.

He locks those blue eyes on mine and says, "My lap is more comfortable than that ball."

Heart hiccupping, I tilt back to get away from him, and lose my balance in the process. He catches me before my butt hits the sand and places me upright on my feet. His soapy scent surrounds me even after he moves away from me. A roar of laughter bellows out of him, so rich and delicious, it makes my mouth water.

"What's got you so frisky this morning?" I take a step back to help me abstain from leaning in to sniff him. *Why is this man's scent so darn appealing?*

Beck shrugs with a wide grin showcasing his mouthful of straight white teeth. "I got a ten mile run in this morning. Guess I'm still high on endorphins."

I grab his wrist and check the time. Four-thirty. Clucking my tongue, I say, "You're a sick, sick man."

"We've still got a while. Let's take a walk." Not waiting for a reply, Beck grabs my hand and keeps it long enough to make sure I'll follow him down the beach.

I sort of wish he'd kept it.

After a few minutes of silence passing between us and the whispering ocean, he says, "Tell me a story, Miss Writer."

"Like last time?" I snicker.

He shakes his head and tsks. "No. You're versatile enough to come up with something different. Give me your best shot."

Oh the challenge. The man knows how to provoke me.

"I'm not ready when it happens. Neither is the sun, for it hides like a coward behind the clouds and stays there long after the catastrophe has inflicted its damage and fled. The intruder shows no remorse, stabbing me until red pours from the wound. The seagulls witness the attack, but flee as easily as the sun when I cry out in excruciating pain. I stumble away, leaving a trail of blood in my wake. The moon shows up eventually and casts a mournful light on the evidence of my misfortune, but it's too late." I wrap up my little story and look over at him as we slowly walk.

"Your murder," Beck answers right away, thinking he has it figured out.

"Now… Aren't you being a bit overconfident?" I sniff. "I was talking about a splinter that got stuck in my foot yesterday."

"How'd you get a splinter?" he asks with genuine concern.

"My deck. I think it's time to have it sanded and refinished."

Beck turns us back around to retrace our steps. "Jack doesn't handle stuff like that for you?"

"Jack? That metrosexual man has weekly manicures. He doesn't do manual labor." My hand flicks out to dismiss the idea. "Besides, I don't expect him to take care of stuff like that for me. I'm a grown woman. I know how to handle things on my own." I want to add that I do most everything alone, but somehow manage to keep that confession to myself.

"Harper, it's okay to not do everything on your own."

It's the last words he shares with me before we meet up with a few class members on the beach. Class goes as usual with me screwing up most all of the exercises, but I don't whine about any of it. I'm too tired to form any words.

As soon as Beck declares the torture done, I waste no time taking my tired behind home. After a shower, the fluffy bed calls out to me. Not up for an argument, I give in. The morning is lost in a deep sleep and feels so good that I'm still dozing in my bed at one in the afternoon.

Cocooned in a sea of white eyelet fabric, I hear a noise coming from the back of the house. Thinking it's the wind moving some of the furniture around on the deck, I roll over and close my eyes. A little time passes before the whining noise of a power tool starts up. Kicking the covers off, I climb out of the bed and go investigate. First thing I notice when I reach the French doors is my deck is clear and all of my stuff is stacked on the sand. I crane my neck to the left and find a giant shirtless man bent over while running a handheld sander against the weathered planks. The phoenix on his shoulder flexes with each pass he makes over the wood.

I step outside and tap Beck on the shoulder. "What are you doing?" I try yelling over the noisy machine.

He flicks a button and the droning ceases. "What does it look like?" He sits back on his haunches.

"But why?"

"It needed to be done. I had the afternoon off, so I thought I'd take care of it." Beck shrugs while his eyes keep coasting over me.

Becoming uncomfortable, I glance down to see what he's so interested in and that's when I remember I'm only wearing a thin, cotton nightshirt that hangs off one shoulder. Snapping my fingers, I say, "Eyes up here."

He looks up with his lips curling. "If you want my eyes to not roam then you need to go put on some more clothes."

Before I can sass back, a familiar voice pipes in,

"That's a man hitting on you, in case you didn't understand, Harper." Jack rounds the side of the house and joins us on the deck.

"Shut up," I say to both of them.

"What's happening?" Jack asks casually.

"Harper's deck needed refinishing. I'm helping her out." Beck stands and places his hands on his hips.

"Need help? I can take my shirt off, too." Jack grabs at the bottom of his light-blue dress shirt like he's about to pull the hem from his slacks.

I pop him in the gut and hiss, "*Jack.*"

"Darlin', you can go topless, too." Jack winks.

Beck grunts.

I snort while stealing a peek at Beck before addressing Jack's sauciness. "You've seen these goods all you're ever going to, buddy."

Beck glares at us and barely stifles a growl. *Oh my.*

"I've not seen the goods since we were three. I think we're due another bath time."

Beck doesn't hold back the growl this time.

My hand darts out and clamps over Jack's mouth. "Never listen to a word this man says," I say to Beck who looks a bit uncomfortable. I then remove my hand and ask Jack, "Does this visit have a purpose?"

"Actually, it does. May I speak with you inside?" All of Jack's saucy tease is gone and is replaced with seriousness.

"Sure." I glance at Beck but he is fiddling with the sander, so I follow Jack inside.

Once the door is closed, Jack looks out toward the deck. "When were you going to tell me?"

"Tell you what?"

"About Beck."

"There's nothing to tell."

Jack turns from the door and tilts his head. "By the way that man watches you, I beg to differ. Seems like a lot to tell."

My arms cross. "What do you mean?"

"Oh, my naïve one, he looks at you like he's seeing way beyond your exterior. And by the way he responded to my banter, he's already claiming some territory."

I glance over Jack's shoulder and see Beck is back to steady sanding. "I thought maybe he was acting a bit weird out there."

"What about you? How do you feel?" Jack asks with sincerity.

I shrug my shoulders and look at the hardwood floor. "It feels like he's gotten under my skin... In a good and bad way..."

Jack's dress shoes step into my line of vision before I feel the warmth of his steady arms circling me. He presses a kiss to the side of my head and whispers, "It's about time you let someone in. I'm proud of you."

I don't know what to say to that, because I'm not sure I've done what Jack says I have, so I keep quiet and allow him to hold me. When he finally pulls back and looks down, my friend looks rather somber.

"What's wrong?"

He huffs. "First off, why in the heck did you have to go and kill off Margo?"

"I just sent the first draft last night and you've already read it?"

"Yeah. Skipped going out last night, because I got so wrapped up in it. Seriously, I'm ticked about Margo. I was in love."

"Someone had to die." I roll my eyes.

"Besides killing my dream girl, I loved it. I could feel the passion of this story. Well done, young lady." Jack smiles but it doesn't meet his eyes.

"What else?"

He sighs long and slow. "Have you watched Roselyn's latest interview?"

"No. I've been busy." The tension begins to tighten along my neck. "Why?"

Jack places his hand on the small of my back and leads me to my office. He places me in front of the computer and with a few dashes over the keyboard, he has the video of the interview playing.

Ten minutes after the interview ends, I'm still sitting here staring at the blank monitor. "She... She was talking about the wrong book..."

Jack groans deeply and pulls at the end of his hair. "If I were here seven years ago, you wouldn't be in the midst of this ghost writing hogwash." His eyes redden. "Harper, it's about to come back around and bite you in the butt."

My head shakes, but I'm pretty sure he's right. "Maybe no one will notice."

"Your fans will. Your publisher will. Maxine sure

as sin better." He starts pacing the room.

Jack has hated the idea of me ghost writing from the time he found out about it, saying I was better than that. And he has always loathed the idea of Roselyn. I've never been able to convince him she's the reason the books sold. He says it's the story itself and that's all me. Not Roselyn.

I do a quick internet search of Roselyn Scott and a bevy of new headlines pop up—several questioning Roselyn's erratic behavior and her fumbled interviews as of late.

Closing out the window, I drop my head in my hands. "What am I going to do?" I mumble and feel Jack's hand rubbing my back.

"First, you are going to hire a lawyer and get that contract of yours gone over with a fine tooth comb." Jack pulls his phone out and begins tapping away on it. "I've got a few contacts. Sit tight this week and let me see what I can figure out."

"Okay."

A few minutes later, he pockets the phone as a slow grin spreads across his lips. Mr. Serious is gone, and looks like Mr. Mischievous wants to come back out and play. "Now here's some advice in the meantime." He pulls me from the chair. "You're gonna take your fine butt to your room and get it covered up. The view is truly nice, darlin', but you need to make the guy work a little harder than this to get to see it."

"He's not seen anything... I was napping when he came up..." My cheeks warm.

Jack chuckles while walking me to the bedroom. "Good. Now go do as I said and when you're done, you need to bring your handsome handy man a glass of water."

"Why?" I pull a pair of yoga pants out of a drawer and slide them on. I grab a bra and T-shirt and close myself inside the bathroom.

"Because I said so," Jack calls through the door.

Once I'm decent, I head to the kitchen to fetch a glass of water like a good little hostess and head outside. Surprisingly, Beck is alone sweeping the sawdust off the deck.

"Where's Jack?" I hand him the glass.

He nods in appreciation, using the back of his hand to mop the sweat from his forehead. "He said something about having a meeting to get to. Said he'd call you later."

"Oh. Okay." I watch him tip the glass to his lips and take a long sip, his Adam's apple working as he swallows. I've never noticed how appealing that part of man is until now. *Hmm…*

"Thanks for the water." He shakes the empty glass to dislodge the ice. Tipping it back, he takes the ice in his mouth and crunches on it.

Taking a break from staring him down like a weirdo, I inspect the deck. It looks quite smooth. "Wow. This looks great."

"I just need to reseal it." He motions to a few gallons of polyurethane.

"How much do I owe you?"

"Nothing." Beck hands me the glass back.

"No. I need to pay for the supplies at least." I tuck a curl behind my ear while eying the paint rollers and sandpaper.

"Okay. You can treat me to dinner."

I almost drop the glass. "What?"

"Dinner." Beck eyes me as he shakes one of the cans like it weighs nothing. "You eat don't ya?"

"Mainly protein shakes and bars." I shrug.

"I've worked up more of an appetite than that. You can take me out." He offers a wry smile.

Is this man asking me on a date? "Umm… I don't normally go out. I'm a homebody, remember?"

"Several places deliver. I'm not picky."

He's not going to let me wiggle out of this, so I head back inside and call Jack. He'll know what I should do.

"He wants to have dinner with me," I whisper while looking through the freezer.

"And?"

"And? What do I do?" I wedge the phone between my ear and shoulder, so I can sort through some frozen diet meals.

"You eat with me. It works the same way with any other man. Promise."

I give up on the freezer, close the door, and lean on it. "I don't think I can go out, though."

"Then stay in, but be sure to keep your pants on. Remember, you don't want to give out free previews of your goods. Keep that bod covered up."

"Jack! You know that's not going to happen. I can hardly handle *this*!" I work my fingers along my scalp, feeling overwhelmed.

"Darlin', I'm in a meeting and have several investors looking at me like I've lost my mind. How about I have something delivered in a few hours. Will that chill your little panic attack out?"

"Okay."

"Okay." He hangs up.

My little panic attack? Jack has no idea. In high school, when everyone was checking off their first date milestones, I sat home alone with quarts of ice cream and bags of cookies. My mom didn't even try to talk me into going to the prom, saying a proper dress would be next to impossible to find in my size. I still feel like that heavy girl, who hid in her room most of her youth, never experiencing a normal social life.

A few hours later, a young guy shows up at my door with large canvas totes from a swanky steakhouse and a flower arrangement.

"Oh, wow. I didn't know y'all delivered." I reach for the bags.

"We don't, but Mr. Calloway called in a favor." The guy quirks his lips and hands me the bouquet.

"Okay, how much do I owe you?" I glance at the entry table for my wallet and try not to think about what he may have read on the card tucked into the flowers.

"It's already been taken care of, as well as my tip. Mr. Calloway said you can thank him by keeping your pants on tonight." The young guy whispers the last part while studying his feet.

Eyes wide, I hurry to say, "I am so sorry you had to relay that. Mr. Calloway isn't right in the head."

"No worries." He waves it off and backs away from the doorway. "Enjoy."

"Thanks. I will... *with* my pants on." This procures a laugh from him.

Closing the door, I head to the kitchen to wait on Beck to get back from his shower. A bad case of nerves hits me suddenly, thinking I could just stand him up, but can't because he's coming here. I place everything on the island and pluck the card from the flowers.

Bachelor Buttons are for celibacy and the mint symbolizes virtue. Darlin', you've held tight to both for twenty-eight years. Let the flowers be a reminder to not get a wild idea to do something you may regret. Love, Jack

Heart racing, I hide the card in a drawer. Jack and his weird morals. The man is always bragging about his wild nights, but acts like my daddy as soon as the first guy comes along and shows me a bit of attention. The entire day is just too much and the bed is calling my name... No, *screaming* my name, so I snatch up my phone to send Beck a text to cancel. Of course, the doorbell would ring at this precise moment.

"Good grief!" I snap at the canvas totes before hurrying to the door. I open the door and find an intimidatingly handsome man. Hair still damp from his shower and smelling fresh as a bar of newly opened soap, the man takes my breath away. Thankfully, he's wearing a plain white tee and black track pants, making me not feel underdressed. I probably should have changed into something cute, but it's too late for that now.

"Hey." He looks me over.

"I'm keeping my pants on," I blurt. Instant heat scalds up my neck and relights my cheeks where the dang things just cooled down.

"If you want to." He grins as he slides his flip-flops off and steps inside.

"Supper just arrived." I hurry back to the kitchen and start opening the containers. Steaks, baked sweet potatoes, and sautéed green beans. I grab two plates and arrange the food, giving Beck both potatoes. With a flourish of my hand I offer him a plate and move to the den. Once I'm settled on the couch, I look around and don't find my dinner date anywhere. "Where'd you go?"

"In the dining room. Where else?"

Oh no. I bet there's an inch of dust on that neglected table. I scoot off the couch and swing by the sink to grab a dish cloth on my way to the dining room. Beck sits with his hands resting in his lap, waiting.

"Pick up your plate," I say and begin wiping the surface. "This room is never used, so I apologize for the dust." Once the table is clean, I toss the cloth on top of the buffet table and sit down with my plate.

"No worries. My family is big on gathering around the table to share a meal. You don't mind sitting in here do you?"

"I'll live through it," I mumble before slicing into the tender fillet and finding it to be a perfect medium rare. "Mmm. This is delicious," I comment around a mouthful.

Beck nods his agreement while chewing. "Here. You gotta try this potato." He reaches his fork with the deep-orange vegetable perched on the end toward my lips, but I shake my head.

"I veer away from carbs."

"That's a good rule of thumb for processed carbs, but your body needs natural carbs. It's all about balance." He keeps the fork close to my lips.

"No thanks." As soon as *thanks* is out of my mouth the potato goes in. "You're so bossy!" I garble out around the bite. Dang, that's sweet and delicious and pairs well with the savory steak. My stomach moans in appreciation for receiving its first real meal in quite a while.

"It's a birthright. I'm the oldest. Can't help it." His lips curl into a smug smile before he takes another bite.

Realizing I've not offered him anything to drink, I hop up and hurry to the fridge for two water bottles and place one by Beck's plate and one by mine. "Sorry, water is all I have." And that's a lie, but I don't think bourbon is a proper dinner choice. I really suck at this hostess crap.

"This is fine."

Remembering his birthright comment, I ask, "How many siblings do you have?"

"Four. One brother and three sisters." He pops a green bean into his mouth and begins chewing. And why is that so mesmerizing to me?

"Wow. That's… a lot."

He chuckles low and thoughtful. "Yep. Never a dull, quiet moment in the McCaffery house."

"I bet not." I huff and keep staring. I absently move the food around my plate while watching him. It's surreal to have a man in my house, sharing a meal and conversation with me. Sure, Jack pops in every once and a while, but this is beyond different.

"Why aren't you eating?" His authoritative tone is back. He pushes the plate closer to me like I'm a flipping two-year-old.

"I'm a grown woman. I'll eat if I want to." I push it away like a rebellious toddler.

"You endured a rigorous workout this morning and you're clearly not getting enough rest. Your body needs fuel." He thrusts the plate back to me. "Eat."

"You're infuriating." I grumble a few more sentiments under my breath before shoving another bite in. "Stop looking at me."

His eyes remain locked on me. "Why, so you can hide food in your napkin like a defiant child?"

"No." I shake my head and push the food around my plate again with my fork, lining the green beans to form a barrier around the steak.

"Harper?" Beck asks, somehow knowing there's more to my answer.

"I can't stand when people watch me eat, like I look like a hog at a trough. Makes me feel disgusting." The last part falls from my lips in a muttered confession as my throat thickens. All of my insecurities flare up, churning the food in my gut in a wrenching pain.

Beck swipes his fork through the sweet potato and offers it to me. When I refuse the bite, he slowly paints the sweet treat along my bottom lip. My tongue instinctively darts out to lick away the mess before it ends up on the front of my shirt. He mimics me, slowly running his tongue over his lip, sending my thoughts into a lustful direction.

"*Nice*," he whispers, ending with a husky groan.

The rest of the meal proceeds with Beck scooting his chair right next to mine and feeding me every last bite on my plate. Never have I thought a man feeding me could be such a sensual experience. The heated meal ends with the ever-present tension the two of us seem to be building on, and I'm not sure how much more I can endure.

After both plates are clean and I'm close to popping at the seams, I load them in the dishwasher while Beck roams around the house. With the much needed reprieve from his presence, the realization hits me what he just did. The manipulative man combatted my insecurities and distracted me by using my lust for him to ensure I actually ate.

"I see you're a Roselyn Scott fan, too," he calls out.

His manipulative tactics are forgotten as a cringe tightens my body. I pad out of the kitchen and find him studying the bookshelf by the fireplace where my bestsellers sit proudly.

"Not really," I mutter out loud, but not meaning to.

"So why all the books?" Beck's brow hitches up in confusion as he points to the shelf.

"Got them as a consolation prize." I shrug. "What do you think of Scott?"

"She's a great suspense author. I've enjoyed all of her novels." He turns from the shelf and faces me.

Wow. The man who's become my crush just confessed he is one of my fans. My skin becomes clammy and my fingertips begin to tingle with the uncomfortableness of it all. I fake a big yawn and eye the front door, hoping the man knows how to take a hint.

He picks up on my brushoff like a boss and hitches his thumb toward the door. "I'm gonna head out. Thanks for supper."

I follow behind him. "I owed it to you."

Beck stops abruptly and swivels around, causing me to collide right into his sturdy embrace. His arms circle around my waist before I can step back, keeping me tucked close to his body. The clammy jitters just did a full-on jig. Gone is any sign of a chill, replaced by a heated comfort. I'm feeling so cozy in his arms that I swear I'm close to begging him to rock me to sleep.

"You owed me nothing." There's a war of apprehension in his eyes. "I'd hoped you had shared the meal with me tonight because you like my company... I certainly enjoy yours."

Swallowing the lump in my throat, I whisper, "I'm just a sassing nuisance. Why would you enjoy that?"

He offers a sad smile. "You don't enjoy being around me?" Clearly, that's the only thing he picked up on with what I just said, and it's not sitting well with him.

A confession wants to be offered, and causes my gaze to drop from his and settle on the dog tags resting on his tight white T-shirt. My fingers trace the metal chain around his neck and on down to the rectangle tags. They are actually warmed from his body temperature. "Beck, you're the only bright moment I've had this week. I… I only went to class this morning so I could see you."

His fingers softly grasp underneath my chin, raising it until there's no choice but to look at him. "I like seeing you there, too. Now… I'd like even more to kiss you, please."

All of the coziness just went to full-blown scorching. My reactions to this man are so bipolar, and I'm beginning to wonder if they make a pill for it.

Beck gently brings his hands to my cheeks and tilts my face toward his. There's a pause before he presses a kiss to my frozen lips. For Beck to be such a rugged man his lips are tender and soft and warm and my body trembles from the perfection of them. I can do nothing but stand here and accept each caress he offers, not knowing exactly how to participate. He begins at the corner of my mouth and languidly works to the other side, lavishing caress after caress along the way.

"Kiss me back, Harper." His words are but a breath, but I hear them.

"I... I don't... I don't know how," I confess and try to move away.

Beck responds by holding me firmer against him while leaning in and softly pressing his lips to mine. His moves are graceful and with confidence as with everything else he does. "Don't make it complicated. It's just a kiss," he murmurs against my lips before demonstrating another feathery pass.

Everything—the humiliation from my lack of experience, the newness of this situation, my trepidation—fades away except for this man's delicate touch. Suddenly, I'm starved for him and should probably be ashamed of myself, but I am too far gone to care at the moment. My hands fist in his hair, another experience I've been fantasizing about in the last few weeks. The locks are thick and beyond soft. Too many overwhelming sensations have my mouth moving with his in a dance of wild abandon.

Beck growls in a deep roar, snapping me out of my lust-filled haze.

Panting, I ease back and ask, "What?"

"You bit me," he says on a low rumble, "but I kinda like it." The gleam in his eyes mingles with his words, and helps to settle the awkwardness trying to overtake me. We both let out a quiet laugh.

"I'm not experienced..."

"We can remedy that," he promises, before leaning down and reclaiming my lips.

This isn't a kiss, but an expression of something beyond our physical contact. His lips are touching mine, but the caress somehow seeps into my skin and penetrates my soul, altering my very essence. I get lost in it and hope to never be found.

Chapter Five

Life likes to play mind games on me, giving me a taste of the goods it can offer before allowing it all to go sideways. I'm living it at this very moment.

"What were you thinking?" Jack's voice echoes his disappointment through the phone.

I move it to the other ear and answer, "I just thought if Maxine could read one of my other stories, she'd see the potential of branding them under a new name… *My name.*"

"Darlin', she's not looking at this from the same angle as you. She's only looking at it from hers. And it says the way she's doing things ain't broke, so don't go monkeying with it."

Maxine's response to the query I sent was a contract for the book to be published under Roselyn Scott, claiming it would help the diva's recent book junket blunders.

"I only sent a few chapters and I'm refusing the contract, so stop yelling at me. I just needed a friend's ear, not a lecture."

Jack sighs long and mournful. "I know. Sorry. I'm just worried about you, darlin'."

The line beeps an incoming call. I pull the phone back and am actually shocked to see Maxine's name across the screen. "Speaking of the devil. I'll call you back." Not waiting for a reply, because truthfully Jack's on the list at the moment, I click over to Maxine. "Yes?"

"Lovely, I'm waiting on you to send the contract back. Time is money."

"About that. I'm declining the contract." There. I stood up for myself.

"That is plain idiotic. How else do you propose you'll get this book published?"

"You're not the only agent in the world. There are millions of you." My voice rises, so I take a long inhale to calm down.

"Yes, and look at how lucky you were to ever get noticed by one of us in the first place. Doubtful that lightning gift will strike you twice."

"I'm willing to take that risk." I take another long breath before pushing it out forcefully. "Your God complex is redundant. I'm sick of being strung along with you only answering a phone when it's in your favor. And I'm sick of you belittling me. I'm done with it." I hit the end button on the phone and toss it on the nightstand before marching to the cabinet for the bottle of bourbon. It accompanies me to the office where I pull up a new page and get lost in the world of fiction.

The skies darken as I figure out how to whittle a happy ending out for my heroine by the end. As it is right now, the poor woman doesn't stand any better of a chance at one than I do.

By two in the morning, the bourbon has

disappeared right along with my heroine's inhibitions. The woman has gone pure wild by running away from her life, helping rob a bank with a filthy-talking guy she met in college, and sleeping with a stranger who may or may not be a soviet spy.

My bleary eyes blink at the muddled chapter on the computer screen in confusion. "Who in the heck wrote that awful crap?" I look around the room for the guilty party, only to find the empty bottle. "It's you." My finger stabs at it as I glare it down. "You better step back, punk." I stand up from the chair a little too forceful, sending it skating across the room, and stumble out into the kitchen where the clock scolds me.

Three hours and I get to see Beck for the first time since he showed me how to kiss. And I'm white-girl wasted.

"This is not good." I groan while scrubbing my hands over my numb face. Maybe some coffee can help rectify some of my wrong, so I fumble with getting a pot to brewing. That gets me to thinking if there's any evidence to this coffee thing or is it just an urban legend, so I stagger back to the office, delete the jumbled mess of a story, and google it. By the time the coffeepot beeps its completion, I've found a considerable amount of evidence to bust the myth.

Only time can sober a person. The liver has to metabolize the alcohol.

Nothing can speed that up, and that really sucks for me. Even though the internet shoots down the coffee, I give it a go anyway.

Four finds me still as drunk as I was when I started in on the pot of coffee, but now I've got a bad case of the jitters on top of it. A wrestling match breaks out with me and my spandex shorts before they admit defeat and get into place. A tank top, sneakers, and a pair of sunshades complete my workout ensemble. I gaze longingly at the tiny golf cart key, but know it's not wise to drink and drive *anything*. The bicycle sounds like a better plan until I fall off the dang thing twice within a few yards from the house. I abandon it by a sand dune and walk a zigzag line to the beach park.

Class has already begun, so I shuffle up beside Nadine and try my darnedest to do the high knees warmup. Falling over a third time, I decide to phone that junk in and manage to just sway in place.

I somehow succeed in keeping out of Beck's sight until halfway through the session. He's bent down and yelling in Nadine's ear, "Get your butt down. It's a plank. Not a downward facing dog!"

"Won't you lay off her for once, you nincompoop," I slur before releasing the plank and plopping down on the sand.

"Watch it," Beck snarls out, but I ignore him and put my head down. "Get up, Blume!" he yells against my ear, his breath searing down my neck.

"Don't feel like it," I mumble without moving. That goes over as well as a fox in a henhouse. Hotshot yanks me up by my armpits, sending the beach into a spin.

"Are you drunk?" He asks, leaning in to sniff for

evidence.

I lean in and sniff him right back. Yum! "Maybe a little. Been a *loonnnggg* night. Say, what brand of soap do you use?"

He releases my arms, looks at me with disgust, and storms to the front of the class. He blows that silver whistle and everyone breaks the plank they were painfully holding. "Ladies and gentlemen, Miss Blume has disrespected the entire group by showing up intoxicated and disrupting this session. She's wasted my time this morning and your money. For that I apologize."

My cheeks are set ablaze and my eyes instantly sting from being called out like this in front of everyone. Thankfully, my sunshades mask it. I feel them all glaring in my direction, but refuse to lift my head to meet any of their condemnation.

"Now. For those *sober* and willing, let's finish with a run." Beck blows the whistle again and everyone starts chasing him down the beach.

Everyone, that is, but me. I turn tail and wander back the other way until I stumble into my house.

Once I'm showered and settled into the quietness of my home, the bourbon sloshing in my veins has settled down.

Slightly sober and beyond ashamed, I go hide.

*****

Darkness... It's seeped in during an untimely

storm that has kicked up just off the coast. The stormy clouds have slung several rain squalls against the shore, shrouding my home in darkness. Hiding behind the couch, the shadows wrap around me like a vise grip. The only reprieve from them is when the lightning flickers through the house, but even that is short-lived. Another prelude of darkness whispers a reminder of my fears.

You're all alone.

No one really wants you.

You'll never be good enough.

The prelude continues until it eases into the postlude of my lowest. The rain pelts against the windows as my eyes stare blankly over the angry waves just outside. I shift on the floor to ease the cramp in my back and cross my legs. The strength of the couch's back is the only thing holding me up. Slouching against it, my fingers absently work the cap of the bourbon bottle in a rhythm of lefty loosy and then righty tighty. The threads clinking against the glass soothe me enough to know the amber liquid is there, but no desire presents itself to take a drink. There's no desire to do anything.

Pounding on the front door entwines with the cadence of the storm. It draws my attention, but not enough to do anything about it. I stay firmly rooted to the hardwood floor, wishing it would soften enough to allow me to sink underneath.

More pounding. "Harper! Open up!"

My gaze holds firm to the temperamental ocean, watching the lightning flicker against the raging waves in staccato glimpses, reminiscent of a strobe light. One vivid flash and then dark and then another flash, but this time the scene causes me to flinch when it presents a monster in front of the glass barrier.

"Open this door!" Beck demands while giving the doorknobs a hasty testing, finding them locked.

Snapping out of my stupor, I lunge for the door and unlock it. Beck rushes in just as a lightning bolt makes contact with a buoy offshore, sending sparks splintering over the turbulent water.

"You're soaked, Beck!" I move so he can get past me.

"Because you wouldn't open the doggone door," he says through clenched teeth, looking downright menacing. "Why were you drunk at five in the morning?"

"Why show up this late? To cast more judgement on me? You wait until dark so no one would see you coming over to the drunk weirdo's house?"

"I've had back to back training sessions today or I'd been here earlier. Almost cancelled them…" Beck shakes his head. "I've done nothing but worry about you all day."

"I'm fine. No worries."

"Drunk at five in the morning is not fine."

"I was up all night writing…" My heart kicks up its pace from feeling ashamed all of a sudden.

"Is drinking some creative vice you use for your writing?" His voice is filled with that drill sergeant tone, demanding the truth.

So I give it to him. "No. It's the vice I use to

combat loneliness." My arms cross as I feel the tears begin to gather in my eyes. I pinch the back of my arm to work up some anger to fight the pity collecting in my chest.

"Harper, you don't have to be lonely." The harshness of his gaze softens as Beck takes a step closer.

I scoff. "Says the man who kissed me last Thursday and has been radio-silent ever since."

"I had to report for duty this weekend in Fort Jackson. Trust me, I'd much rather been here kissing you than training a bunch of whiny recruits."

"Whatever."

Beck lets out a heavy huff and bends to meet my eyes. "Would you stop hiding behind that wall of sass and attitude for once and really listen to me? Ever since I've met you, you're all I see. Your sharp wit, your spunk, your thoughtful expressions when you watch people. You think you're hiding successfully, sometimes angling behind Nadine. Know this, Harper Blume, you're all I see."

My eyes drop to the floor and notice a puddle forming around his feet when another flash of lightning ricochets around the room, so I hurry to my bathroom to retrieve a towel. The squeaks of his shoes follow close behind me as the rumbling of thunder shakes the earth.

"Is the power out?"

"No." As I pull the towel from the linen closet the light comes on, nearly blinding me. Shielding my eyes with the towel, I mutter, "Too bright."

"Are you still drunk?" He pushes my hands down and inspects me.

"No." I blink a few times to adjust to the sensory overload. And I'm not talking about the light. Beck McCaffery dripping wet with that scowl on his face is the most sensuous sight I have ever seen. Clearing my throat, I whisper, "Take your shirt off."

With his turquoise eyes trained on me, Beck reaches a hand back and whips the shirt off in one fluid motion. He tosses it in the sink and takes a step forward.

Silence blankets us with only a rumble of thunder interrupting it every so often as I mop the towel along his broad chest and then down over the well-defined plains of his torso. He bends forward, grasping my hips for support while I drag the towel through his hair.

"Turn around," I manage to croak out.

He actually listens, so I continue to dry him off. As the towel treks along the phoenix on his shoulder, the jagged surface of his skin underneath the ink catches my attention. Dropping the cloth, my fingers reach out and test the texture. "Beck…"

His hand reaches over his shoulder and comes to a rest on top of mine, pressing it into the camouflaged scars. "Roadside bomb, but I survived it. It's just another part of me that makes me who I am." He sounds so indifferent about it, but that scar had to have come from a nightmare full of pain and suffering.

The most natural need washes over me, so I act

on it without thought and press my lips to the phoenix. Our hands move aside to allow me free reign of the scar. By the time I've kissed every jagged inch of the scar, I'm trembling with some foreign emotion.

My lips move to the valley between his shoulder blades as I inhale the clean scent of his skin. I lean my forehead there and watch my fingers coast along the taut muscles along his back.

Beck remains statuesque, allowing my exploration. The only movement is the pronounced rise and fall caused by his heavy breathing.

"I've never seen a man's body before," I confess while my hands come to a rest on his hips.

Beck slowly turns and looks down at me. His eyes are considerate instead of judging. "Never?"

I shrug. "Only in pictures."

"So you've never *been* with a man?"

My head offers a timid shake. Who knows why I've decided to admit this to Beck, but beyond my understanding I have no desire to lie to him.

A groan rumbles from the back of his throat as his eyes grow heated. "You have no idea how appealing that is."

My cheeks heat up. Wanting to run from the awkwardness, I hurry to the closet and fish out a pair of Jack's jogging pants from the stash of clothing he keeps here.

"These okay?" I hold the pants out, but Beck hesitates with accepting them.

"You just happen to have men's jogging pants on

hand?"

"Jack keeps some here. You know, in case of an emergency." I keep to myself that Jack sometimes crashes here. It's none of Beck's business anyway.

He considers this before nodding his head slowly, causing the drying locks of his inky hair to fall over his forehead.

I step a little closer with my hand reaching out to brush it back, but freeze from the trepidation overwhelming me. Before I can chicken out and make a run for it, Beck captures my wrist.

"It's okay, Harper." He brings my fingers to his mouth and presses them to his lips as he toes off his shoes.

Beck leans down and removes the soaked jeans but keeps his boxers on. Before he can step into the jogging pants, I kneel and inspect the scar marring the skin beside his left kneecap.

"What happened?" I ask as my fingers skate across it.

"Humvee caught fire during a motorcade attack. Took me a while to get one of my men out of the back, so my knee got cooked." His words come out in a raspy whisper.

Another booboo I wish nothing more than to kiss back to better. My lips replace my fingers and slowly caress the blemished skin. A vicious clap of thunder seems to be rushing me, but I refuse to listen. I am so drawn to this man, it frightens me.

After I have given the scar on his leg proper attention, I squeeze my eyes shut and slowly stand. I hear him wrestle with pulling up the pants, but don't dare peek.

"Open your eyes, Harper," Beck says quietly after a few minutes pass.

I do and find him gazing down at me. He reaches out and pulls me close as he claims my lips in a searing kiss. We kiss until it becomes unbearable.

"Beck..." I huff out against his lips.

"I know." His hands drop as he takes a step back. After a few deep inhales, he says, "It's time for bed."

I'm about to walk him out when Beck sweeps me off my feet and carries me toward the den.

"It's only eight," I comment after glimpsing the time on the alarm clock.

"Yes, but you need a good night's sleep." He settles into the thickly cushioned rocking chair and cradles me close to his bare chest. "You make me tired just looking at you." He traces underneath my eyes with the tip of his finger.

Tears tickle the back of my throat. "I am tired," I whisper after coughing them away. "Tired of a lot of things."

Tired of the loneliness. The dark holes whittling away at my insides. The not knowing how to belong in this world...

"Well, let's start with some sleep and then we can figure out how to handle the rest. Okay?"

I want to know why Beck would even want to be around a loser like me, and why he's not thumping me over the head with his Bible for the drunken stunt I pulled today. I ask instead, "Why are you doing this?"

"To show you you're not alone."

I sit up and try untangling myself from him, but his arms lock down and end the attempted escape. Wiggling, I mutter, "I don't want your pity."

"Good, because you're not getting it. Hard as it may seem, I like you. And for reasons I don't even understand, I enjoy your sassy mouth."

His statement makes me want to sass some more, but I tamp it down and settle back against his warm chest. "Fine, but you can stay only until it stops raining. Then you gotta get lost."

"Why?"

"I won't be the reason for you breaking your holy rules." I'm grouching at him, but snuggling closer as I do. *I make no sense.*

"What rules would these be?" Beck asks while running his hand through my hair.

It's all I can do to stifle a moan and my eyes start rolling around like they're drunk again. "Fornicating. Sleeping with a woman." I finish the hogwash with a yawn, knowing we're doing neither.

Beck chuckles so deeply I can feel it rumble through my body. It's a comforting feeling I could burrow into.

"You know we're doing nothing wrong here."

"People won't know that."

"I don't care what others think, and neither should you." His hand moves from my hair to my back and begins drawing lazy circles along my spine.

I think I dozed off but snap back to when he says,

"God knows my intentions toward you are mainly innocent."

My head pops up. "Mainly?"

"I wouldn't mind making out with you."

Beck's grin is so severe, I have to duck my face to the crook of his neck to hide from it.

"Not happening," I mumble against his warm skin, even though the idea does sound appealing.

"I know. Rest. I got you, okay?"

I nod and snuggle closer to him as my eyes drift shut. The storm has calmed its rage and has hushed down to a calming rain shower. I listen to the pattering sound it makes along the tin roof. The melody of that, combined with the slow rock of the chair and Beck's even breaths, lulls me into a deep sleep without me noticing it.

Chapter Six

Late morning arrives and finds me alone in bed, but a new scent lingers on the linens. I bury my face into the pillow that still holds the indented proof he was here and take a deep inhale. If it wasn't for this alluring smell I'd swear last night was only a scene my overactive imagination conjured all on its own. Sometime before the sun woke up, Beck placed me in bed. After I begged, he laid down for a little while.

I sprawl under the tangle of the white fluffy bedding, not wanting to leave the tender memories dancing through my thoughts just yet—him rocking me, soothing me, lying beside me with a mile between us. His gentlemanly gesture makes me smile, and I'd be happy to stay in this very spot and cling to last night all day long.

"Are you sick?" Jack asks, sending me bolting up in the bed.

"What? NO! You scared the heck out of me! You have got to stop doing this sneaking up junk!" I push a palm to my chest and glare over at him where he's leaning against the bedroom doorframe.

"Your cheeks are flush. You sure you don't have a fever?" Jack stalks over and places his hand against my forehead and then to my cheeks. "You're clammy."

I bat his hand away and climb out of the bed. "I'm fine. Go make some coffee and I'll be out in a minute."

"Coffee's already made." His right eyebrow cocks up in suspicion.

"Oh... I must have set it up last night and forgot. My mind feels a bit foggy." I shift my weight from one leg to the other and fiddle with the hem of my nightshirt.

"Yeah? I found a full bottle of bourbon behind the couch. You wanna talk about it?" Jack reaches out for a hug.

"No!" I dodge around him and lock myself in the bathroom. Leaning against the door, I take a deep breath before opening my eyes but clamp them right back shut when the first thing they land on is Beck's shirt still resting in the sink.

After I get over it, I nerd out and go sniff the dang thing. Sure enough, the fresh soapy scent of him continues to cling to it.

"You're such a jezebel," I mumble to the mirror. The reflection of a wild-eyed, tangled-headed woman glares back at me.

Pulling my act together, I hide the shirt in the hamper and work on washing the heat from my face. A few splashes in, I give up and jump into a frigid shower. The icy pelts do the trick and soon the chattering of my teeth is the only thing I can focus on.

Once I'm presentable in a pair of jeans and a blouse, I head out and find Jack perched at the kitchen island with a cup of coffee in hand. I slide onto the stool beside him and pick up the cup waiting on me. The robust aroma is as heavenly as the first silky sip.

"Thank you." I lean my head on Jack's shoulder, hoping my affection will help him forget my bizarre behavior from earlier.

"You can thank me by going to a party with me tonight." He takes another sip from his white mug. It's the same color as all my dishes. "There's going to be a live band."

"So not my scene." I roll my eyes and sit up. "I'm gonna pass."

"Darlin', you need to get out of this house and be around other humans." He throws his hand up to stop me before I get started. "Exercise class and the liquor store don't count."

I cross my legs and angle more toward him. "I get out more than that." Not much more, but the food market and bank count.

We go back and forth on my recluse problem, as Jack calls it, before moving to the perpetual thorn in our friendship side. Maxine and the cage she has snared me in. After two more cups of coffee each, we've come to no conclusions.

Rinsing the cups, Jack asks, "So... you do anything interesting last night?" He gives me a sidelong glance, making me fidget.

"Umm..." Memories, that were quite *interesting*, flash before my eyes. "Not really," I lie with a shrug.

"Mm-hm. So nothing but an untouched bottle of

bourbon got you through the storm?"

My shoulder twitches up again like it's suddenly come down with a case of Tourette's. "I just wasn't in the mood to drink it... Actually, I was still hung over from showing up to boot camp yesterday morning wasted." I decide to mix a little truth with my fibs.

"Oh, I bet Sergeant Sexy got ahold of your lush behind for that." There's a weird gleam in his brown eyes.

I stutter out a laugh and shrug again. "Yes, the jerk called me out in front of the entire group."

"Seems he's forgiven you." Jack presses a kiss to the side of my head as he pulls a crumpled piece of paper from his pocket and slides it onto the counter in front of me. "Found this by the coffeepot. I'll be back at eight to pick you up. Be ready."

Before I can unglue my mouth to apologize, he's out the door. I look down at the note.

You're not alone. I think last night was enough proof. I wouldn't mind a repeat. ~Beck

Sitting here, I'm torn between grinning like a goofball over my first note from a guy and grimacing like the rotten friend I am for lying to my best friend. I grab my phone from the bedroom and text Jack. *Sorry. I really suck for lying to you.* His message pops up immediately and I know I'm forgiven when I see he's twisted my words to form his own response.

Jack – *Not gonna lie... U really do suck.*

Me – *See u at 8.*

Jack – *Wear something sexy. ;-)*

Shaking my head, I make my way to the closet in hopes of finding something that'll get a rise out of him and not in the way his saucy mind would have wanted.

*****

"Ah, heck no. Go back inside and change." Jack closes the passenger door of his Audi before I can crawl in. The silver sports coup is just a sleek as its owner.

"What's wrong with this?" I gesture at my attire, tearing my attention away from the car's beauty and directing it to the equally beautiful man leaning against it with his arms crossed.

"You look like you're heading to the baseball stadium to catch a game." He glances at his flashy wristwatch. "Hurry up."

"It's either the jeans and baseball jersey or I'm not going." I cross my arms defiantly.

"What about the ball cap? Can you lose that at least? I have people I want to introduce you to tonight."

"Nope. It stays, too." I reach up and adjust the brim of the hat.

The standoff lasts longer than I would have guessed. Our battle of the clothes and hair goes round after round for a full fifteen minutes before an exasperated Jack throws his hands up and admits defeat.

We are complete opposites tonight. Jack sleek in a black dress shirt and grey slacks with me casually rumpled in loose jeans and oversized jersey—him broadcasting his attractive perfection with me hiding my unappealing flaws.

The ride to the party is quiet and holds just enough tension to allow my nerves to get the better of me. "Jack, this probably isn't a good idea."

"I know it's not. You might as well show up naked, 'cause that's how much attention you're going to draw to yourself by looking like this." He waves in my direction as he pulls the car into the valet parking area.

"What?" I grouch out.

"You think this baggy mess is going to be your shield. Darlin', you failed. Every person in that club is going to give you one look and will instantly wonder what you're hiding." He puts the car in park and runs his eyes over my frumpiness once again. "How in the heck did you even manage getting all that hair underneath this hat?" He taps the brim.

Before we can continue the argument, a guy dressed in a black T-shirt and black jeans opens my door and offers a hand to help me stand. The handsome redhead eyes me curiously before releasing my hand. I don't miss the exchange between him and my driver, but don't comment. I guess Jack pegged my lame hiding attempt correctly.

We walk up to the steel and glass beast called Vel where Jack is part owner. Beams of blue and purple lights shine against the palm trees swaying in the breeze. Their shadows dance against the building in time with the music vibrating through the outdoor speakers, allowing the long line of partiers waiting to get inside a sneak peek of what's to come once they ever make it past the threshold.

Jack shakes hands with a massive guy guarding the door. "Bryant, how's the night treating you?"

"Great, man. The house is full." The dark-skinned giant looks at me, but gives nothing away with his hard features.

"That'll make the night interesting." Jack slaps him on the shoulder, laying his masculinity on rather thickly. He places his hand on the small of my back and leads me into the most crowded perdition I've ever ventured into.

Before I can freak completely out, a brightly colored cocktail in an otherworldly blue hue is shoved into my hand. Downing it in one long gulp to avoid the sickly sweet taste, I hand the empty glass over only to receive a hot-pink replacement. As I'm tugged through the throngs of bodies swaying to the pulsating beat, glass after glass of weak alcohol find their way to me. I think I'm going to end up with a stomach ache from the high doses of sugar before the traces of alcohol can offer me a buzz.

Dizzy and slightly nauseated, I keep my head down and focus on my Converse sneakers. Jack tries introducing me to a few people, but a blur has crept into my vision. Loud music and laughter collide, making it impossible to focus in one direction. He remains my anchor for about an hour before letting go of my hand and that's when I lose him in the sea of bodies. One moment he's by my side, the next I'm cocooned on an upper dancefloor among sweaty strangers who seem in a dancing trance.

This is not me and not my kind of place. The only place I belong is back at the cottage in my dark office cave.

A set of arms halt the escape I was about to make, pulling me against a chest. "You look like a treat needing to be unwrapped, sexy!" a man yells into my ear.

My elbows shove backwards, making contact with the stranger's gut until he releases me.

"Feisty! This is gonna be fun." He bellows in laughter.

I swing around and find a bleach-blond man who's barely an inch or two taller than me. Mr. Napoleon makes up for his limited height with lots of cocky attitude. He's squinting to the point that only a sliver of pupil peeps from each eye and his cheeks are rosy. Clearly he started hitting the spirits a little too early.

"No fun here, man. I'm *mean!*" I bare my teeth for effect, but the dude laughs at me and grabs at my waist with one hand and starts tugging at my hat with the other.

"Come on, sexy. Take that hat off and let me get a better look at ya."

Thick blonde curls fall all around my face once the hat disappears. He sloppily brushes the mass of hair out of my eyes.

I see red.

The adrenaline starts to burn through my veins, pushing out pure evil as my fist balls up and takes a swing. His face isn't nearly as soft as I thought it would be and has my entire hand throbbing.

"No one touches me!" I shout.

Blood starts trickling from his bottom lip as he dabs at it in disbelief. "I think I'm in love," he lisps out, sending the onlookers into a raucous roar of laughter.

Rolling my eyes, I give him a harsh shove and stomp off. I yank my phone out and text a death threat to Jack, promising to dismember him piece by piece and toss his remains in the ocean, before rushing out of an exit.

The tears threatening to spill seem to dry in the sultry breeze as I take a deep inhale of it. Pushing the breath out, I suck in another long gulp and repeat this breathing technique until the tingling along my arms and the pounding in my chest settle down to a manageable attack.

"You okay, little lady?" a vaguely familiar voice asks.

I glance way up and find the bouncer I met at the door earlier. *Bryant was it?* My head nods as I keep to the deep breathing.

"You need me to get Jack?"

My head shakes. I keep breathing.

He considers me through several breaths before grunting. "All right. How about a cab?"

My head nods vigorously with hearing the best option of the night. *Inhale through the nose. Out through the mouth.*

Not much time wastes until I'm tucked inside the back of a cab and am heading back to my safe haven, vowing to never leave it again. It's a short ride, but gives me enough time to reflect on the stupidity of Jack's decision tonight. What was he thinking bringing me into something so wild and swarming with people?

One way to break a skittish animal, throw them in headfirst?

That saying flickers through my fuzzy mind and I shake it away. Wrong. So wrong. Five years it took to guilt me into an excursion such as this and one hour to determine it will never happen again.

The cab delivers me home in mostly one piece. With my missing hat and throbbing knuckles, I'm a little worse for wear. Before I can dwell on that too long, a dark shadow moves on my porch.

"I ain't in the mood to kill a man tonight, but this gun will do what it's gotta do!" I try growling out the threat, but it comes out with a hint of slurring.

Beck's chuckle washes over me like a soothing caress, sending my tense shoulders back below my ears. I stumble up the walk and take a seat on the step beside him. The entire club debacle seeps away at the sight of him lounging beside me, looking like he just hopped out of the shower and strolled over here. From his damp locks and sweatpants, I'd say that's exactly what he did.

"Where've you been? A ballgame or something?"

"Or something. Jack guilt-tripped me into going with him to a dance club."

"Yeah? You went dancing dressed like this?" He tugs at the hem of my jersey.

"I didn't dance. I had a hat on at one point, too, but some jerk swiped it."

"Harper?" There's a mix of warning and concern in the pronunciation of my name, but it's still poetic coming from his lips. My eyes focus on that mouth until he repeats, "Harper?"

"The entire night's experience was a nightmare. Do you go clubbing?" I ask even though I'm pretty sure of his answer already.

"Not my scene."

"That's what I said." A breeze sweeps across the porch and sends my hair all over the place. Beck gently combs it from my face, his blue eyes holding a hefty amount of concern.

"Why did Jack push you to go to a place like that in the first place?"

I shrug. "Jack thinks it's his job to yank me out of my shell."

Beck drops his hand and huffs. "Well, I can think of a better place for that than a club."

"Oh yeah? Where?"

"Church," he says instantly and I instantly recoil.

Scrunching up my nose, I mumble, "Not my scene either."

"Why not?"

"Fakers aren't my idea of fun company." There's

no holding the flinch back over my own words, knowing I'm as fake as they come in my professional life.

"How do you know that if you don't go to church? You shouldn't knock something until you've tried it." His dark brow hitches up.

"Oh, I tried it for eighteen years. Trust me, I have plenty of evidence to knock it."

"What evidence is that?"

A few golf carts come zooming by with a crowd of teenagers hooting and hollering at each other. After they pass, I'm ready to present my case. "The church I attended picked certain parts of the Bible to fit their lifestyles. Twisting other parts so they could feel entitled to judge and condemn others who didn't fit into their religious mold."

"Explain the mold," Beck states as soon as I pause to take a breath.

"The mold where it was okay to consume several slices of cake along with an extra plate of cookies and brownies at the church social. They had no problem with members making pigs of themselves and doubling the size of their temples. But heaven forbid if a member is caught at a restaurant having a glass of wine with their meal. That somehow didn't fit the mold and the bloated members would come up with a plan before the next service to show the outcasts to the exit."

Beck nods as though considering what I said. "Anything else?"

"Plenty!" *Oh, I'm just getting started.* "Don't you

dare say a curse word even though that's nowhere in the Bible, but it's perfectly okay to talk about the person who slipped and said the ugly word as long as you call it prayer request instead of gossip. And it was even better if you follow the gossip session with a "bless their hearts" before you say amen."

"Overindulging seems to be the issue here. They thought it was okay to overindulge in some things but not others, correct?"

"Yep." I nod, impressed he gets my point. "Anything in excess is considered a sin from what I gather from God's words."

"So, you have no trouble overindulging or maybe slipping with some inappropriate words every now and then?"

"I see where you're going. Yes, I overindulge. I was over two hundred pounds not too long ago, and you already know I can get carried away with a bottle." I point at my chest. "You won't find me sitting on a cushioned pew pretending I don't, so don't try turning this religious crap around on me"

"What's really the point in going to church?"

"Beats me!" I push a heavy huff out with growing frustrated by this stupid conversation.

"I go to church to praise God and give Him the respect He deserves for blessing me with this life."

"I'm good there."

"Explain."

"I don't live much."

"You're the only one to blame for that."

"How so?"

"It's your life, Harper. If it's unwritten, then pick up the blame pen and get to it."

"I don't know how," I whisper.

"You need to start by dealing with your insecurities and quit deflecting that by blaming that church of yours or any other person." I try to interrupt, but Beck plows on. "Answer me this. Do you like people holding your mess-ups over your head?"

"No, but—"

"Then stop doing it to others."

"Can we just drop it?" I snap. Huffing and crossing my arms, I direct my scowl to the dark beach house across the street. It looks so all alone. I can relate.

"Okay," he mutters, sounding like it's not okay with him at all.

Silence settles around us for a while, but the breeze picks up and starts teasing me with hints of Beck's scent. I can take only so much before leaning in and inhaling the fresh scent permeating his long neck.

"You just sniff me?"

"Yes. You always smell so delicious." I steal one more lungful of his comforting fragrance before straightening back up.

"Are you drunk again?" There's weariness in his voice and it doesn't set well with me that I put it there.

I flick my left hand to shoo his accusation away. "No. Jack kept shoving sissy drinks in my hand, but I'm fortified with top-shelf bourbon. And the little buzz I had going on back at the club has been burned away from the adrenaline."

"Adrenaline from what?" Now he's sounding agitated.

I shrug dismissively and secretly sigh in relief that we've veered away from the church subject. "From the fight." I probably shouldn't poke at this bear, but it sure is fun to get him riled up.

"Level with me. I'm not playing this silly game." Drill Sergeant McCaffery has arrived.

"You're no fun... Okay, so the guy that stole my hat thought it was okay to grab me. I taught him a lesson."

"I hope you taught it to him firmly. Or do I need to go over there and hunt him down?" Beck is already about to stand, but I wave him to stay seated.

"I punched him in the mouth and made the punk bleed. I took care of him myself."

"Atta girl." He produces his knuckles for a bump.

Without thought, I bump his and a pain ricochets from my knuckles and on up my arm. "Oww!"

Beck brings my hand over to his lap and inspects my booboo. "It's swelling. Let's get some ice on it."

"I will later. Let's just sit here a little longer, please."

"We can hang out inside while I ice your hand." He's got that authoritative glint in his eye.

"No. I..."

"It works better the faster we get the ice on it."

"No." I refuse to budge from the step and he looks close to lifting me against my will.

"Why not?"

"Because I don't want you to come inside tonight." I expect him to ask *why not* again, but he remains silent with his eyes seeking the answer. He's so intimidating and I'm close to chickening out, but I manage to deliver the truth. "I just need some alone time. Tonight was overwhelming... Last night was overwhelming..."

"You know that just makes me want to stay even more."

Now it's my turn to ask, "Why?"

Beck sits back down and runs his hands over his face. "You have my protective instincts on high alert. All the time."

"I can take care of myself." My chin juts out and he reaches over and captures it with his fingertips.

Leaning down, he says against my lips, "I didn't say you couldn't, but I want the honor of doing it for you."

Well, what does a girl say to that?

Not a dang thing, I tell ya.

I seal my lips to his and kiss out my fears, my hopes, and my exhilarations over Beck's declaration. As we continue to kiss, I feel his fingers slip into my front pocket and grab my house key.

I lean my head back to sever the connection. "I'm serious about you not coming in tonight."

He says nothing, just gets up and goes to unlock the door. We both stand at the threshold waiting. For what? I haven't a clue.

"Beck, if you come inside, my brain will turn to

mush and I may do something stupid…like bite you again…or punch you."

This cracks the tension and we both let go of a small laugh.

Beck hands over my key and graces my lips with another kiss. "Get some ice on that hand, Rocky."

He gives me an appreciative smile, looking proud for some reason, before stepping off the porch and into the night.

I lean against the doorframe and watch on until his form completely disappears. One thing I've grown to admire about this man is he knows when to push me. He also knows when to step back and allow me a breath.

Taking a much-needed deep breath, I head inside to tend to my bruised hand.

Chapter Seven

Google is said to be my friend. Maybe so since it tells me what I need to know, even if it's not normally what I had hoped to hear. I tap out my question at four in the morning with one hand while my other one throbs like a toothache, hoping it'll be kind this time.

Q. - How to treat bruised knuckles?

A. - Initially, ice and anti-inflammatory meds. Exercise to help relieve stiffness in the joints.

Nope, not what I wanted to hear. I shut the computer down and text Beck while shuffling into the den. *My hand hurts.*

He texts back—*Come on anyway. We'll work around it.*

I glare at the phone and toss it on the couch before plopping down beside it. Sure, I want to see his handsome mug, but I've woken up with not one ounce of aspiration to work out today. I lean my head back and start dozing off when the phone comes alive with Justin Timberlake's "SexyBack" crooning from the tiny speaker. My left hand awkwardly picks it up, making me feel right pathetic.

"What?" I grouch into the receiver.

"I'm outside waiting on you," Beck answers as a

knock sounds at the door.

Groaning, I stand up and head over to open it. "I don't feel good. Can't we both just stay here?" Once the door is open, I end the call and stare at him. He's in a black T-shirt, black cargo shorts, black hat and sneakers. "Are you going to a body boot camp funeral?"

His lip twitches as he pockets the phone, but doesn't allow me the gift of a smile. "Yours if you don't go get dressed."

"I don't feel up to it today." My nose wrinkles as I show him my hand.

Beck gently presses his lips to my purple knuckles before spinning me around. "Get dressed. You don't want to make me late. Now hurry." He reaffirms his demand by popping my backside.

I hop out of the way and slice him a glare. "You're the devil."

"And you're certainly no angel. Get the lead out, Blume!"

"Sir, yes sir!" I give him an exaggerated salute and stomp to my room.

After wiggling into a pair of loose jogging pants and an oversized T-shirt, I open the door and plow into Beck's chest.

"Watch out before you hurt yourself some more." He takes my shoes out of my good hand and bends down to put them on my feet. After he ties them, he yanks the drawstring tight in my pants and ties that as well. "You got one of those hair tie things?" He looks up in all sincerity.

And I look down and crack up into a fit of giggles. "You're going to do my hair?"

He stands and hurries into the bathroom on a mission. "Yes, or you could ask one of the women in class to help you out when we get there."

I move him out of the way to open the drawer below the one he was plundering through and pull a tie out and hand it over. "Guess you're stuck with the honor. None of them will even look in my direction."

Beck carefully gathers my wavy mess of hair, using his fingers as a comb. "Because you're trouble. If you'd behave they'd probably be friendly." He manages to wrangle my entire mane into a low ponytail.

"Not bad." I eye the lumpy hairdo in the mirror.

"I have three sisters, remember?"

"That's right."

He checks his watch. "We're cutting it close. Let's go."

Mr. Bossy-pants tugs me through the house and out the door, slowing just enough to grab two bottles of water from the fridge.

A dark-green Jeep Wrangler sits idling in my drive. Oddly enough, it's the first time I've seen him drive anything anywhere. "I thought you normally walk or bike to class."

Beck lifts me into the passenger seat that has no door and fastens me in with the seatbelt. "Normally I do, but I thought you would need a lift this morning." He cracks open one of the bottles of water and hands it over before hurrying to the driver's side. "Drink some of that before we get to class."

He's all business, so I do as I'm told and sip water for the two-minute drive to the beach park. It takes longer to get me in and out of the Jeep than it did to actually drive it.

Beck remains all business throughout the class, shouting out orders in his usual alpha male tone, but his eyes never stray from me for very long this morning. I receive no special treatment from him, but he doesn't call me out when I skip over anything that would have me using my right hand. No planks, burpees, or push-ups for me today, which is why I think he concludes with a four-mile run. This effectively wakes my mouth up, and I protest for miles 1 through 3.

Mile 1...

"Really? Running again?" I yell from the back of the group.

Mile 2...

"Did we pay this jerk an obscene amount of money just to run around the beach like a bunch of idiots?" I screech a few feet back from the group and kick at the sand for good measure.

Mile 3...

"You're phoning it in, Coach Boring!" I yell and am about to stop altogether when Beck doubles back and starts pushing me into a running pace.

"Either shut it, Blume, or we double it to eight miles!" He shoves me none too politely and barks out, "Move it, move it, move it!"

Between his threat and the death glares from the

others, I keep my lips sealed during the last mile and *move* it.

As everyone gathers their bearings and water bottles, Nadine takes a step in my direction. It's quite noticeable the brunette has lost a considerable amount of weight in the last two months. Hard to believe the McCaffery torture is almost complete.

"This morning was tough," she comments before taking a long pull from her water bottle.

I look over my shoulder to see who she's talking to, but no one is there. "Umm... yeah," I reply, hoping she is in fact talking to me.

"Your hand looks awful. What happened?" She steps closer and looks it over.

I try flexing my fingers out, but the pain begs me not to try that again for a while. "Bar fight," I say, and then sniff with played-up attitude.

Nadine snorts. "You're a nut."

"Is that why you never speak to me?" I scan the ocean as the sun starts dancing along the top of it in a soft peach hue.

"No. It's because I'm scared if I do, you'll get me in trouble during class and I'll have to run or something else equally as torturous."

We both laugh at that, even though it's the truth. "So, why talk to me now?"

"Beck suggested it. He thinks we have a lot in common and would make good friends. I think he may be right from what I've gathered over the summer."

That sends my eyes on a quest to find him. He's

speaking with a group of guys from class, but has his sights set on me. We give each other a quick nod before I turn back to Nadine.

"Confession, I've never had a girlfriend," I mumble, embarrassed by this truth.

"I'm married, and I don't kiss girls." She holds her hands up with her declaration.

I huff a small laugh. "You know what I mean."

She smiles, and the expression lights up her face. Really looking at this woman for the first time, I'm struck by her understated beauty—eyes that match the hue of her brown hair and sharp cheekbones that are beginning to really show off with the recent weight loss.

"Yes, I know what you mean, but I can hardly believe such a lively character as yourself doesn't have bookoodles of girlfriends."

Taking the last sip of water, I toss the empty bottle into a beach receptacle. "Why's that hard to believe?"

"You're hilarious. The last two months have been the most entertaining months I've had in a long time."

"Well now… You've made my morning and now I need to treat you to coffee." I hear myself suggesting and can hardly believe it.

"Sounds good to me. I've got another hour before my husband leaves for work and I'll be back on mommy duty. There's a coffee shop a few streets up from here."

"Yes, but I live closer. We can sit on the deck and chill for a while."

"Sounds even better." She grins while looking over at Beck. "I noticed you had a ride this morning, but I can drive you home."

"Okay. Just let me tell him and I'll be ready to go." I skip over to the picnic table where Beck is collecting his belongings. He bends forward to grab his mesh equipment bag, and it's the perfect angle for me to plant a kiss on his stubbly cheek.

He straightens and offers a small smile. "What was that for?"

"Just thanking you for wanting to take care of me even though I can do it myself." He has no idea how it's pulled at my heart for him to take the time to seek a friend out for me.

"Well, that's a relief. I figured your mean fist would be teaching me a lesson after that run." His right eyebrow quirks up.

I ignore his jab and plow on, "Look, Nadine is going to give me a ride home."

"Okay."

Thinking we're done, I turn to walk off, but he hauls me back by the hem of my shirt. Before I can protest, the man lays a kiss on me that wipes my brain clear of any vocal skills.

"I want to see you later," he demands against my mouth, and I love how he does that, not even talking will get in his way of kissing me.

I manage a dazed head nod.

"Inside your house this time," he clarifies.

Before I can shake my head in defiance, Beck releases me and saunters off. Danged if that man just didn't take another part of my soul with him. He keeps this up and he'll own the whole darn thing.

"I didn't just see that," Nadine stutters from behind me.

Still watching him walk off, I mutter, "Uhh…" Not quite a word but getting there.

"Shoot. That means I lose the bet," she grumbles, breaking the trance.

"What bet?" I ask, turning to eye my new friend who may not be from what she just admitted.

"Most of the group has a bet going on that by the end of this course one of two things will happen. Beck will finally reach his limit with you and kill you off, or lay claim to you like a wild caveman."

My eyes narrow. "And you were on the murder side of this bet?"

She holds her hands up and then motions toward a grey minivan in the parking lot, so we head in that direction. "Only in the beginning, but they wouldn't let me switch sides once we shook on it. And the killing is a little exaggerated. It's more on the lines he finally kicks you out of class."

"It's that serious?"

"Oh, yes. The losers have to treat the winners to that pricy seafood buffet on Main Street. Looks like I'm paying up."

We climb in after Nadine clears the passenger seat that's littered with animal crackers and small toys.

"Why? We've got a few more classes and he's not dragged me off by my hair yet."

Nadine snickers as she maneuvers the van out of the parking lot. "Now that would be a sight."

"Take a right and it's two blocks on the right." I pause for a second, but can't help asking, "What brought this ridiculous bet on in the first place?"

"The two of you look at the other like you either want to choke or kiss the other to death."

I know that's exactly how I feel most every time I'm around him. "Humph. There's still some time left. My disappearing isn't out of the question just yet."

"It'd save me fifty bucks. I would appreciate that." She grins. "I've got to know, do you make it a habit of getting drunk and crashing fitness classes?"

"Only when I'm bored," I deadpan.

She hoots. "That was priceless. I had to pull out my dusty military training to keep my composure so I wouldn't crack up at your silliness."

I glance over at her and see the grin is still plastered on her face. "Was I that bad?"

Nadine flicks her eyes to me and then back to the road. "Beck had us doing squats at one point, but you were in your own little world doing some funky dance move instead."

I scoff. "Nu-uh. I don't even dance."

"You were that morning and wearing sunshades before dawn!" She shakes her head and swats my arm teasingly. "I think you were doing something called the butterfly. Your legs were going in and out and your head was bobbing to music no one else could hear." She giggles while wiggling her shoulders in mock dancing.

"I sure am glad I don't remember any of it." I roll my eyes and look out the window. "One more house up."

Nadine parks the van in my driveway and gazes out the windshield at the white cottage. "Cute place."

"Thanks," I mumble, feeling awkward receiving a compliment. Why is that such a hard thing to do, anyway?

Once the coffee has brewed, we gather a cup each and plop down in the lounge chairs on the deck.

"Ahh… Now this is the life. Let's trade." Nadine sips her coffee in contentment.

"My life ain't all it's cracked up to be. Trust me."

"And what exactly is your life?" She looks over at me in interest.

I try shrugging the uncomfortableness off my shoulders, and mumble, "I'm a writer."

"No way. That sounds so… romantic."

I release a loud snort. "Romantic? Hardly."

"What is it you write?"

"Novels." I can't believe I didn't fudge the truth, and it feels good to own it for a change.

"So you get paid to create fictional worlds?"

"I guess you could say that."

"Romantic."

"Whatever." I sling out my go-to word and turn the tables on Nadine. "Beck mentioned you were in the military. What branch?"

"Marines."

"No way. You're a Marine?"

"Was."

"Once a Marine, always a Marine." I look at her in admiration. Nadine is obviously one tough cookie. "Now that has a romantic air."

"Please." She huffs out a nervous cough, not liking the attention, and I realize we've got a lot in common.

"Say, how would you feel about allowing me to interview you?"

"For what?" She takes another sip of coffee.

"A book I'm toying around with where the heroine has a military background." Truthfully, I've been brainstorming the story all summer since meeting the enigmatic Sergeant Beck McCaffery, but I want the woman in the story to be the soldier.

"Oh, well, that could be neat. But I don't have much free time. Between raising my babies and trying to get back into shape, there's very little time left." She inhales slowly, before whispering, "Plus, I make a good many trips home to check on my little brother… He has cancer."

"Oh… I'm so sorry to hear that." I reach over and grasp her forearm, hoping it offers her some comfort.

"Thank you." Nadine smiles. "He's tough, so I know he will beat it."

We grow silent and remain in it for a while as I study Nadine in my periphery. She worries her lip and gazes out at the beach in deep thought. It's clear she needs a reality break. When she tries hiding a sniff, I decide to push the interview idea once more.

"We can meet for coffee before your husband goes to work once or twice a week. I'd really like to have a real-life heroine help me bring to life my fictional one." My fingers are already itching to get started.

"I'm no hero, Harper." She shakes her head, finishes the last of the coffee, and sets the empty mug on the table between us.

"Nonsense. Isn't it true you toughed it out in Iraq for not one but two tours?"

"Yes—"

"That settles it. I've got myself a war heroine!" I hop up, retrieve her empty cup for a refill, and go grab a notepad and pen.

The hour goes by way too fast, but ends with Nadine promising to come by after class next week. As the minivan pulls away, I close the door and head to the office in excited awe. Beck isn't the only one with battle scars. A sniper missed Nadine's heart by mere centimeters and the lady lives to tell the tale.

My pen is still scribbling over the notepad when a knocking starts up against the front door at dusk. Tossing the pen down, I flex my aching fingers a few time and head to the door. I pull it open and see Beck standing there in a blue V-neck tee and faded jeans.

"Want to pen a scene in your life tonight?" He follows the question with a killer grin, sealing my fate.

I'd go wherever he leads right at this moment, but retort, "I'm not big on socializing. Had my fill of that nonsense last night."

"What if I promise it'll just be the two of us?"

Realizing I'm still standing by the door gawking

at him instead of inviting him inside, I step back and wave Beck in. He brushes a sweet kiss on my cheek before walking past me. "I need to grab a quick shower so make yourself at home." I point to the den but halt at the door of my bedroom. "What should I wear?"

"Doesn't matter. Shirt and jeans." Beck shrugs before settling on the couch.

I hurry through a shower, work some serum in my damp hair to combat the frizz, and go with jeans and a lacy tank top.

"That was quick," he comments when I rush back to the den.

"I'm not high maintenance." I slide my feet into a pair of flip-flops and follow Beck out the door.

"Good to know." He walks me to the Jeep and opens the passenger door for me.

"You have doors now?"

"Yeah. I put them back on this afternoon, since I'm going to have a passenger from now on."

"You are?"

He leans in and takes care of the seatbelt for me. "That's my plan and I need to keep you safe," he whispers in my ear before placing a soft kiss there.

Stunned, I sit here and watch him close my door and maneuver around the Jeep to load up. No words come to me until he's pulled out of the driveway and has us heading inland.

"Where are we going?"

"You'll see."

Twenty minutes later, I *see* we've parked beside a

secluded pond in the country.

"Parking? Really?"

Chuckling, Beck reaches behind my seat and produces a basket. "Picnicking."

"Oh."

He reaches back again and hands me an old quilt. "Will you carry this?"

"Sure." I gather the worn blanket in my arms and scoot out of the Jeep and into the balmy night. The air feels thicker out here. I take a deep breath, and instead of the usual briny scent, the air is infused with an earthiness. Notes of murky water and freshly mowed grass mingle in the breeze.

While I gaze around, Beck leads us over to the pond bank.

"How do you know about this place, Mr. New-to-Town?" I ask as he helps me spread out the quilt.

"I personal train Nadine. This is part of her property. She suggested it when I asked her earlier where to take you for a picnic." He sets the basket down and starts unloading plastic containers.

"You asked her?" I cross my arms and look around at the fairly large pond. It's shaped similar of a kidney bean and has a small dock on the other side.

Ignoring my question, Beck points to the quilt. "Sit." He settles down beside me and hands over a fork. "Mind if I say grace?" he asks.

Before I can answer, an owl hoots out from somewhere in the midst of the patch of woods surrounding us. I giggle and bow my head, not really caring one way or the other.

"Thank you, Lord, for this woman who you've allowed to crash my life. Thank you for this time we have together and for the food. Amen."

I lift my head and see Beck doing the same, feeling peculiar about him choosing to thank God for *me* of all things. My lips remain glued until realizing he's just piled a paper plate full of food and is shoving it into my hand.

"No way. I can't eat all of this." I try shoving back but he releases it and starts fixing his own plate. The moon and stars are bright enough I can see the contents clearly—shrimp salad with cherry tomatoes and cucumbers and a generous scoop of fresh fruit. "Where'd this come from?"

"My kitchen." Beck pops a shrimp into his mouth and then digs around in the basket, producing two bottles of sparkling water. He hands me one and takes a long pull from his.

"You made this?" I set the bottle down and take a nibble of shrimp. The hints of dill in the creamy dressing pairs well with the juicy seafood and before I know it I've put a good dent into the mound on my plate.

"Yes. My mom taught me how to cook at a young age, saying the true way to a woman's heart was food and not flowers." Beck takes another bite as he scoots even closer to me, blocking out most of the breeze. He seems to always be in some protective stance around me, making me feel safe.

"Funny you say that. Jack has been giving me flowers since I was no more than six years old." I test some of the fruit and discover honey drizzled over it, making the treat even sweeter.

Beck glances at me and then back to his plate. "You'd rather have flowers?"

"From Jack, sure, but he's not trying to find a way to my heart."

"You've never been more than friends?" He looks back at me, skepticism pinching his forehead.

"Why do you keep questioning that?" I drop my fork onto the plate and set it down.

Beck reaches over and hands it back. "I'm just trying to figure out how much of a chance I have with you." He points to the plate. "Eat."

"I consider Jack my gross big brother, but love him enough to pick him over pettiness any day." I'm not sure if Beck is a jealous kind of guy, but I won't be putting up with it.

He smirks. "The things he says to you don't sound very brotherly to me."

"Jack mouths off because he knows it embarrasses me, but he's harmless." I keep picking at my food to pacify him while listening to the crickets chirping. I've gotten so used to the sound of waves roaring a low hum at the cottage that all of the noises out here are quite interesting. "So, what's this scene supposed to be about tonight?" I wave my fork between us before spearing a strawberry and popping it into my mouth.

Beck takes my plate and places it in the basket with his before stretching out on his side. Propped up with one arm he reaches over with the other and pulls me until I'm mirroring him. Smiling, he says, "This scene is where the beautiful blonde falls for the charming boy."

"Please." I roll my eyes, knowing he's nailed the scene on the head, except for the part where I'm beautiful and there's certainly nothing boyish about him. I've already fallen for him. That happened at least two chapters back.

He grasps my hip and drags me closer, the moon casting a glow to his aqua irises. "You don't find me charming even a little?"

"Maybe just a little," I whisper right before his lips connect with mine, but I draw back. "You sure this scene isn't about making it around the bases, because I can tell you right now I'm not *athletic* enough to make it off home plate." I give him a sharp look, hoping to emphasize my point.

"Oh, I bet I'm skilled enough to help you make it safely to first base. In fact, we've already made it there a few times." He takes to skimming his lips over my exposed shoulder and then on to my neck.

"First base is as far as we're going," I warn as his lips edge to the corner of mine, sending my heart into a fit of nerves and excitement.

"That's fine." He licks my bottom lip, sending a tingle to ignite there and skirt down my spine. "But just so you know it only gets better."

"How do you know?" I stutter out, my hands grasping onto his broad shoulders as he rolls me to my back.

Beck kisses his answer until the night is swirling

around us. Languid and tender is his touch, reassuring me that, yes, it gets better, but promising me to not take it any further.

I'm lost in this kiss until the wind disappears. Everything stills around us and then my skin comes to life. Slapping the invasion away, I try and fail to remain in the romantic scene Beck has written for us.

"Ow!" I slap at my neck and elbow him in the process. "I'm getting eaten alive!"

Beck jumps up and helps me to my feet while slapping at his forehead. "Man, I didn't even think about bug spray."

I glance around and find the air swarming with millions of blood suckers. Stings ricochet all over my back. Hopping around and brushing my arms wherever they can reach, I screech out in pain. Beck grabs me up and hauls me to the Jeep in a mad dash. After I'm safely tucked inside and away from the mosquitos, he backtracks and gathers the basket and quilt.

He climbs in and slams the door, causing it to bang in frustration. Clearly, the pesky insects ruined his plans. I can't help but giggle when he faces me, revealing several red welts blooming along his face. One in particular in the middle of his forehead looks like a horn trying to emerge.

"This isn't funny." Beck glares while scratching at a welt on his cheek.

"You know it is," I rebuke, scratching at my neck.

"But I still want to kiss you some more." He growls out, sounding like a brute.

"What's stopping you?" Before I can sass some more, Beck lunges over and sends my seat reclining backwards.

His heavy weight settles against me as his lips pick back up with mine where they left off. We kiss until both of us seem to not be able to ignore the irritating bites any longer.

Growling, he sits up and starts the Jeep and reluctantly leaves our scene behind.

"What are you over there snickering about?" Beck asks as he drives me home. My mind is caught on a replay of our date as I stare out the window. "Tell me," he says a little louder when I don't respond.

"What we did... Isn't that... That's something teenagers do, right?" My neck and cheeks heat, but I can't control the grin on my face no matter the embarrassment. I've never been parking before. He can deny it all he wants, but that's what we did. My window still holds the foggy evidence.

He gives me a devilish grin in return. "I think we did our scene justice that some dumb teenagers wouldn't be able to pull off."

Beck sounds so sure of himself that I have to laugh. "Teenagers would probably remember insect repellant."

"Who says that wasn't part of my charming plan? Forget the spray to lure the beautiful blonde inside my Jeep?" Beck tries pulling off a smug expression, but the red welts totally ruin it.

Laughing, I lean over and place a kiss on his cheek as he parks in my driveway. "Thank you for helping me pen an experience I missed out on as a teen."

"The pleasure was all mine, ma'am. I'd like to pen several more scenes with you soon."

I'm not ready for the scene to be over so I ask, "Would you like to come inside?"

"That's probably not a good idea. I may do something dumb like bite you or chase you to second base."

"Fair enough." Disappointment mingles with relief.

"But I'd like to walk you to your door."

I toss my hands up. "No. Stay. If you walk me to the door, I may do something dumb like drag you inside."

Laughing, Beck leans over and offers me one last kiss for the night. I worry he's becoming my new vice. Not sure if that's any healthier than chocolate or bourbon.

"I'll see you soon."

"Soon," I mumble and head inside alone. For some reason, that's really starting to bother me.

Chapter Eight

Soon. The internet defines this word as meaning within a short period of time. Two days is too long to be considered soon to me. This fact has left me cranky and with my first bout with writer's block. Beck said he'd see me soon. Even sealed his promise with a sweet kiss. The sucker lied. Now an inner irritation has joined in with the itchy spots on my skin. I rub at a lingering bite on my forearm as I stare absently at the ocean sparkling before me. The ebb and flow of the waves keep my attention until heavy feet hit the deck.

I look up but quickly go back to studying the ocean. "What do you want?"

"Nice to see you, too." Beck chuckles. He takes the lounge chair beside mine and yanks mine closer. "Hold my hand, Miss Grouch."

"I will *soon*." I cross my arms and refuse his request.

"Did you miss me?" Beck asks with too much laughter in his tone.

"No. Truthfully, I think you're unhealthy for me and should just leave me alone."

"How's that?"

I sit up and glare over at him. "I'm a writer. I

need to write. You've bossed your way into my life and have wreaked havoc on my routine. This kissing me and then going MIA for days at the time... I ain't got time for that."

"I had this two-day body boot camp to instruct with a few other guys. Sorry my routine doesn't revolve around yours, Harp."

"Oh, now I'm harping on you again?" I plop back down in the chair and close my eyes.

"I'm flattered you miss me."

Before I can open my eyes and glare, Beck has wedged himself in the chair with me. I push against his chest. "Get off. You're blocking my sun." Dang. He smells so good that my arms wrap around his neck to draw him nearer. Ugh. Here goes the tug-of-war with myself again.

He skims his nose along mine. "I missed you, too. Let's work on a new scene today."

"I need to be writing some scenes. Alone."

Beck places a feather-soft kiss on my pouty bottom lip. "Are you on a deadline?"

"No, but—"

He deepens the kiss, effectively cutting off any excuse I could have come up with. "Hmm... I love kissing you." His confession has my toes curling. "Go somewhere with me, please," he says against my lips and then goes back to kissing my refusal away.

When he finally draws back enough to eye me, I'm breathless and want nothing more than to go wherever he leads—to the end of the earth, to the coffee shop, to the garbage dump... "Where?"

"You'll see." Beck pushes the dark locks back from his forehead and stands. He offers his hand and helps me up, too.

"Cut-off jeans and this T-shirt okay?"

Beck motions to his pair of jeans and V-neck tee. I think he favors that style due to his thick neck. The man is all muscle. "We're good. Let's go."

After we load up and he begins pulling out of my driveway, I try again. "Seriously, where are we going?"

Beck glances at me but quickly goes back to studying the road. "Worship service."

"Wait. What?" I grab his arm. "I'm not dressed for church. You can't just spring something like this on me!" I worry my bottom lip between my teeth and look around for an escape route. I'm seriously about to freak out! "My mother would have a conniption fit if she knew I showed up to church in jeans!"

"You're dressed just fine. Stop harping."

"I'm not harping. This isn't harping. I can show you harping!" I let go of his arm and deliver a punch. "What type of church is it?"

"The normal kind." He downshifts and rolls to a halt at the red-light.

"What do you mean by *normal*?"

"Why do you question everything to death? Harp, harp, harp!" Beck shakes his head and takes back off a little faster than warranted, sending my head to bounce against the headrest.

Crossing my arms, I fix him with a mean look. "If your plan is to take me to some kind of new age religious crap, then you need to let me out right now." This is what I get for declaring I'd go anywhere with him. I'd rather go to the garbage dump!

Beck pulls into a beach access lot and yanks up the emergency brake. Taking this as my cue to blow this scene, I fumble with opening the door. Before I can scoot out, Beck reaches over and tugs me back in and pulls the door shut.

"It's Oceanside Baptist Church. Happy?"

Refusing to answer, I let out a huff instead.

"For someone not into church, you've got quite a high standard in place."

"I'd rather not go to any church, but I certainly don't want to go to some weird one."

"As long as the church stands on Jesus being our Savior, it doesn't matter what the wrapping looks like. And it certainly doesn't matter what title graces the sign in front of the church." He rubs the back of his neck, his tell for being frustrated. I've seen it enough in the last month to call it. "You do realize there won't be a religious police at the door of heaven asking to see your church denomination license before allowing you in, right?"

Sure, Beck has a point, but I won't admit it. "I don't appreciate you not being straight up with me."

"For that I apologize. You're just too fun to get riled up." He leans over, engulfing me with his soapy aroma and body heat, and places a gentle kiss on my lips.

"I'm not sure that apology was believable," I sass before he draws away.

Beck's aqua eyes sparkle. "Guess I should give it another go." He brushes his fingertips along my cheek and reclaims my lips. Tender at first but it rapidly grows with intensity.

The kiss Beck lays on me clears any transgression the man has ever committed against me.

Grinning, he sits back into his seat and releases the emergency brake. "Now we're going to be late, and that's *your* fault."

I'd rather we skip the whole dang thing, so I offer, "Need me to apologize now?"

Beck shakes his head and releases a low chuckle. "Later. I'll be sure to collect."

Once he makes it through one more stoplight, Beck pulls into another beach access lot and shuts the engine off. I crane my neck around, looking for a church, only to find a pile of rubble beside an open air pavilion across the road from the beach. People line the wood benches underneath.

"That's the church?" I ask, not believing it.

"Yes. Their building was lost in a fire a few months back, but they still meet every Sunday morning."

"Oh. I think I remember hearing something about that. How'd you find it?" I give him a sidelong glance before going back to looking over my shoulder where the people are singing.

"Heading to breakfast one Sunday morning. I stopped at the light and could hear them singing, so I joined in."

I'm impressed that he would just take initiative to

just join in a service. No way would I ever do such a thing. I'm not very fond of the idea at this moment either.

"Do you make it a habit of crashing church services?" I tease.

"No, I make it a habit of praising God any chance I get. I've moved a lot, but I always try to find a church family wherever I end up."

That's way too much interaction with unknown people and it makes me slouch down lower in the seat, wishing it would tether me to it.

Beck must sense my hesitation. "They're a really cool bunch. Come on." He's out the door and on my side in a flash and is pulling me alongside him across the street before I can slam on the brakes.

Thankfully, he picks a back bench and no one seems to notice us crashing their service. They continue to sing with no musical instruments to accompany them. Beck joins in but I choose to people watch. It's quite an eclectic group with a mix of races and a wide range in age. Some are dressed casually, some in their Sunday best, while others are a bit out there. While the group seems filled with opposites no one seems to oppose anyone's company.

When the song wraps, I wait for one of the gray-headed men wearing a suit to step up to the small wood podium up front. Instead, a bald-headed guy sporting a dark hipster beard takes the post. His attire is simply a pair of dark jeans and an untucked white button-down shirt.

With his hands shoved inside his pockets and an

air of casualness about him, the guy looks over the group of maybe a hundred or more people and says, "Good morning. I see a few new friends have joined in with us today. My name is Mason Townsend and I'd love to share God's word with you for a little while." He flips open a worn Bible and begins reading.

I tune the words out and get distracted by his facial expressions. The guy is quite animated. Each time he makes a point, Mason looks up and arches an eyebrow in an impressive upside-down V. How in the heck does he send the one up to where his hairline is supposed to be while the other remains hovering over his eye like it should? He could give the Rock a run for his money with the dramatic eye arch thing. I don't realize I'm trying to mimic him until Beck taps my leg.

He leans over and whispers, "You got something in your eye?"

I blink several times and shake my head. I'm about to go back to studying Mason's expressions when he suddenly breaks out singing the chorus to a familiar hymn. Oh, wow. The man can sing. And just as suddenly as he broke out in song, he's back to speaking. He now has my undivided attention. Never have I seen such in a worship service.

Back at my childhood church, the services were always stuffy with the preacher looking down his snarling nose at the congregation, mainly speaking in a snippy tone and raising it occasionally to wake some of the members back up.

Not Mason. He speaks with the group and not down at us. He asks questions and expects comments in return. He makes jokes and laughs, but in the next breath grows somber in such earnest that I can't help but feel empathy. It feels like he's leading a conversation with everyone. It's comfortable. This unusually normal guy standing before the group has drawn my interest enough to want to listen to see what he has to say.

Mason flips a few pages in his Bible and begins reading. "Restore unto me the joy of my salvation." He glances up with that one brow arching dramatically and nods his head. "This thing called life. Yeah, it gets tough sometimes." He motions around the open air pavilion and then over to the scant remains of the burnt building. "Hello! You get me right?"

Several folks speak out in agreement.

"We need each other, but it's impossible unless we're going to be honest. Don't show me your false self. No sir. Take off the mask and let's get real with one another." Mason steps around the podium and begins strolling down the makeshift aisle. "It's the only way to truly restore your joy. You can't pretend the bad away!" His voice rises on the last part and sends a pressure to build in my chest.

As I watch the preacher move back to the front, I try rubbing the odd sensation away. It's an uncomfortable disturbance inside me. Foreign and out of place and I want nothing more than to be rid of it.

"Something wrong?" Beck whispers close to my ear.

I keep my eyes forward and shake my head.

"You sure?"

I nod and drop my hand back to my lap only for Beck to pick it up and entwine our fingers. I can feel him watching me for the remainder of the service, but keep ignoring his scrutiny and the achiness of my chest and the thickening of my throat. I wonder if I'm coming down with something. I pretend to scratch my cheek to test the heat level and find it to be quite warm with possibly a fever.

It's on the tip of my tongue to tell Beck I need to go home when Mason asks for everyone to rise and sing "Amazing Grace" while opening up the altar for prayer needs. Surprisingly, Beck lets go of my hand and makes his way to the front where several others are kneeling. Not being able to stand another minute of this, I scurry back across the street and hide out in the Jeep.

Closing my eyes, I rest my head against the window and try to calm down. Mason's words about pretending to be something you're not hit home and I'm reeling over how miserable it's made me. Taking a calming breath that stutters in and right back out, I ache to be free of the mess I'm in. I'm halfway through a set of breathing exercises when I hear the other door open.

"What's wrong, Harper?"

I open my eyes and see Beck leaning over me with concern reflecting in the pools of blue. Not liking it, my eyes drift back shut.

"Headache. Just need to get home please."

"Okay."

The engine comes to life and is followed by the sway of the Jeep moving. When it stops and I hear the familiar clicking sound of the emergency brake being pulled up, I finally reopen my eyes and climb out.

"You want me to come in?" Beck asks before I shut the door.

"No. I'm just going to go lie down for a while."

"Can I come over later?"

"Umm…" I focus on the front door in its soft blue hue. It begs me to come on. "I need to work some."

"When can I see you again?"

A huge part of me wants to throw caution to the wind and just let my façade crumble to my feet, but the more dominant reclusive side of me screams to keep that baby in place. To keep the world out where it belongs. Away from the ugly truth lurking just below my surface.

"Come on, Harp. Let me see you," Beck tries again, and something about how he words his plea seals the deal.

Not wanting to be seen, I glare at him and say, "Soon." Leaving it at that, my weary body hurries to get away from him and all the weird feelings he's helped stir up in me this morning.

I don't know what to make of it and I sure as heck don't like it. Surely, I'm coming down with something. In no time, I have the computer on and have looked up the symptoms for influenza. I skim over the list. No fever, but a flush hits my skin each time I think about this morning. A sore throat is listed. Sure, with every swallow there's an unpleasant tightening, but it's not quite sore. I perk up when my eyes land on fatigue and lightheadedness. Those two I definitely have going on.

I grab my phone and shoot Jack a text. *Trying to fight off the flu. Need stuff for home remedy.*

Jack – *Lemon and honey?*

Me – *Yes. I've got the bourbon. Hurry.*

With that taken care of, I close out the internet window and pull up one of my works in progress. The hope is to lose myself in a story, but I end up rereading a paragraph about a hundred times without taking it in. Beck and that flipping service continue to hold my thoughts in some unsettling trance.

"Honey, I've got the honey!" The sound of Jack's nasally voice somehow snaps me out of the trance.

Pushing away from the desk, I head to the kitchen where the clanking of silverware leads me to him. He's already hunched over a cutting board slicing lemons.

"You sound like the one needing medicine." I swipe a lemon wedge and suck all of its bitterness away.

"Summer colds are the worst." He wrinkles his perfectly straight nose that's a bit red on the end.

"If you'd stop kissing so many summer *girls* you'd keep your health more intact." I toss the lemon rind into the trash and grab the bourbon and two tumblers out of the cabinet.

"For the record, I've not kissed a summer girl in over a week." Jack nods once as if proud of the declaration. He muddles the lemon with a few sprigs of mint before adding the bourbon and a generous amount of honey.

Summer is Jack's playtime and always has a vacationing beauty on his arm. Before they can check out of their condo rentals or hotel rooms, he's normally checked in with another woman.

"Probably because you kissed and got yourself too sick to kiss another." I push into his shoulder with mine.

"Is that what you've done? Too much kissing? You don't look sick to me?" He eyes me suspiciously.

I swallow dramatically and release a puny cough. "I feel sick."

Jack sniffs like he doesn't believe me, but hands over the medicinal drink anyway and takes a sip from his own glass. "Let's go sit and be sick together for a spell. I'm beat."

We make it to the couch and plop down, both of us seeming to be exhausted. "You need to slow down, Jack." I reach over and comb a curl away from his forehead with my fingers. It's the same curl I've combed for most of our life and it's the main way I show him affection.

"No worrying over me, darlin'. It's just the cold wearing me down." Jack finishes the rest of the fiery drink, releases a hiss, and sets the glass on top of the end table. Mere seconds pass before his head falls on my shoulder and he's snoring.

Settling in for a longer spell than planned, I sip the home remedy until it effectively numbs out the heavy pressure from my body. We both end up camping out on the couch until Jack disappears before sunrise.

His concoction did such a good job Sunday afternoon, I give it another go Monday and by Tuesday I feel back to normal. I even make it to class with only minimal dread, but the tightness and ache invades me again when Beck spends the entire session staring at me with soft eyes. He never looks at me with soft eyes while training us and it weirds me out.

Before he can completely get the word *dismissed* out of his mouth, I dart over to the golf cart and will it to turn into a speed demon and get me away from this confusion stirred up inside me.

"Harp!"

I hear Beck yell my name, but pretend I don't...

Wednesday rolls around and it feels like Monday needs to be repeated just to make sure the dreadful cold isn't trying to show back up, so the last of the medicinal beverage disappears along with all my cares...

I make it to class Thursday a little worse for wear. Apparently, a steady dose of the medicinal remedy can leave one a bit hungover. Either way, I'm able to avoid Beck for most of the week and keep the achiness at bay. I call that a success.

It was working fine until Beck demands I see him outside of class today. Each text he sends, I offer the same snippy reply stuck on repeat. *Soon.*

Sitting in my office with a blank word document in front of me, I finish texting soon once more. The bubble appears on my phone screen with his reply immediately following.

Stop harping on SOON. Enough! I'm coming over after this training session. I'll be there SOON!

I'm about to send a message to tell him to kiss it when the phone begins an obnoxious ringtone, the theme music for the wicked witch from the Wizard of Oz. The one that plays every time she's either on her broom or a bike.

I answer it with dread. "Maxine, what can I do you for? You need my blood for Roselyn's DNA now? Or is she in need of her assistant? I'm pretty good with an iron."

"There are definitely some wrinkles that need your assistance with ironing out. I've booked you a flight and a driver is on the way to take you to the airport."

Well, this sucks.

Chapter Nine

Some chapters in life seem to be made up of too little time. My summer enduring Beck's brutal boot camp has felt oddly brief, like the chapter didn't give me enough and has only left me wanting more.

While some chapters feel unreasonably short, others just feel too darn long, dragging on and on with no end in sight. The dread of giving up on it or seeing it to the end wars through my mind. This dreadful weekend in New York has been precisely that. Several times I've thought about skipping out on this chapter altogether and heading back home to hermit away.

Sitting behind the curtained partition that separates me from a panel of authors participating in a Q and A at the Mystery Suspense Convention with a headset nestled among my unruly curls, I continue to be a puppet in this charade. Maxine has full control of my strings, but that control is about to be severed as soon as we fall over the precipice we've been teetering around for far too long. The impact is going to leave one nasty bruise, but it's time.

A fan directs a comment to Roselyn, bringing me out of my thoughts. "You've managed to write an assassin with such charismatic wit that you've made me fall in love with him. Tell us how Fritz came to be."

"Oh, I just love Frazer, too."

"Fritz!" I hiss into the mouthpiece to correct her blunder.

"Fritz, I mean! There are too many characters dancing around in this noggin of mine!" Roselyn coos out, eliciting a round of laughter from the audience.

"Fritz was developed from a charming friend of mine." I pause to allow her to convey this and then continue, "My friend is quite vulgar most of the time, but wraps it in just enough southern charm that I always forgive him." I pause again so she can repeat and then conclude the answer with, "Of course, I took my friend's raucous quirks and multiplied them by a million to create Fritz. He is, by far, one character I truly enjoyed seeing come to life. Too bad he kills for a living."

Once Roselyn adds a little spice to the answer, the crowd chuckles again and seems content to move on to another author. My afternoon drags by with me feeding the lazy woman her answers and her repeating them in her flirty vernacular.

I cover the mouthpiece after one particular question about the plot that Roselyn had no idea how to answer, and direct my scowl at Maxine who's sitting beside me backstage. "Isn't it stated in her contract that she has to read the dang book before its release?"

Maxine shakes her head. "I don't know what's gotten into the *both* of you lately, but I'm fed up with the attitudes and poor effort."

"Us?" I cough. "This is all on you and Roselyn. Not me. My contract states all I have to do is write the Breakers Series and give you first option. Nowhere in there does it say I have to do mess such as this!" I wave my hands around, taking in the cluttered backstage where boxes of books and swag wait for the book signing portion of this event.

"Your contract?" She eyes me over the top of her hot-pink glasses.

I have the sudden childish urge to pull a tendril of hair that's sticking in a silver halo around the hussy's head, but restrain myself.

"Yes. My lawyer has gone over it front to back, as well as Roselyn's. And I'm here to tell you right now, this next book is the final installment in the Breakers Series. I'm done with you after that."

Maxine balks at me, her lips flapping like a suffocating fish, but no words come out.

Jack's lawyer has spent the last month going over the contracts with me and his advice is to walk away from the series and start fresh. Easier said than done, because those books will always be my babies even though I may never have custody of them. It's the price I have to pay for my writing freedom, though. Sadness hits me square in the stomach, but I breathe through it.

Staring at Maxine's cold eyes, the decision is becoming less burdensome. My bones already feel lighter with finally telling her how I really feel.

"I'm on a plane back home after this," I tell her

while half-listening to the Q and A in my ear.

"Not so fast. Adrian Wild has requested a meeting with us Sunday evening."

"That means I won't make it home until Monday? No. Tell him it's today or never." I hit the off-button on the headset and sling it across the room.

Maxine's eyes track to where it lands, but makes no move to go retrieve it. "We're not in a place where we can make such demands at the moment."

"Why not?" My arms cross as the anxiety coursing through my veins heats up.

"Have you not noticed your cut from Wild Idea Publishing hasn't reached your bank account yet?"

Truthfully, Beck has become such an unexpected distraction this summer that I have no idea if there's a penny in my account. The statements are by the computer, but they've been neglected.

I shrug a shoulder and start collecting my notes when the applause breaks out on the other side of the curtain. "What's up with that?"

"I'm not quite sure. He's been so rude in the last month, not returning my phone calls. Ignoring my emails and messages…"

"No kidding? That's got to be pretty bitter, being served a dose of your own medicine." I sling my messenger bag over my shoulder and head for the back exit.

Sharp claws pinch into my upper arm, halting my retreat.

"How dare you treat me like this after everything I've done for you. Where's all of this attitude coming from?"

I yank my arm free from her grasp and pin her with a look of revulsion. "What about everything that I've done for you? And how about we talk about the way you've treated me?" I take in lungful of air and let her have it. "You've made me feel from the very beginning that I wasn't good enough to represent my own stories. You made me feel less of a person, like you were doing me a favor. Sure, you may have, but I've made you an incredibly rich woman and one of the top rated agents in this country. So how about offering me an apology and a thank you."

When the stubborn woman remains silent, refusing to give an inch, I march out the door without looking back.

"This chapter is dragging," I mutter to myself while watching the flight schedule. It taunts me, laughing at my delusional hope of getting a last-minute flight home. The airport is a cacophony of people hurrying to get on with their lives. Some rushing to the terminal while others, such as myself, have been shackled to a hard plastic chair. We are halted in limbo, wanting to be somewhere else but are at the mercy of that dang flight board.

My phone is the only company I've had in the last two hours and I've ignored it like a boss. Maxine has filled my voicemail. I've deleted her rants and pleas without a second thought. It starts up again with the neutral ringtone as the announcement for another departing flight that I couldn't get on is delivered. I pull the phone out to send the call straight to voicemail, but an unknown New York number flashes on the screen. Interest has me answering.

"Hello?"

"Miss Blume?" A young man inquires.

"Yes?"

"My name is Oliver Kasen. I'm Mr. Adrian Wild's assistant."

I scan the airport and mumble, "Okay."

"It's come to Mr. Wild's attention that Sunday is inconvenient for you to meet with him, but he's out of the country until then."

"Okay."

"He sends his apologies, but is also adamant that you be in attendance at that meeting."

Career suicide whispers through my thoughts, halting the idea of telling the young guy where his boss can stick it. Recalling my first encounter with Adrian Wild, I feel like he may end up being my ally, so I start trudging out of the airport and mutter a third, "Okay."

*****

I'm an idiot. An absolute idiot. The internal scold keeps repeating as Maxine and I sit across from Adrian Wild's ultra-modern desk, feeling like two unruly kids in the principal's office. Instead of being expelled for our iniquities, we've been fired.

"Come on, Mr. Wild. Surely a few slips come with the territory." Maxine pastes on one of her maniacal smiles, but Adrian doesn't waver.

"A few slips? You keeping the ghost writing situation from me is not a minor slip." He steeples his fingers and narrows his eyes. "Roselyn didn't even read the last book, did she?"

"She's—" Maxine begins.

"You ladies are becoming sloppy." Adrian directs his focus on me with a look of discernment etched along his face. "What I don't get is why you aren't representing your own work in the first place."

"Harper is deathly shy... It's the only way we were able to get this to work," Maxine jumps in again, delivering the half-truth.

Adrian keeps his eyes fixed on me. "I asked Miss Blume."

Clearing my throat, I mumble the only thing I feel like saying at the moment, "I just want to write."

Silence blankets the office for a spell, until Adrian finally says, "Well, I wish you the best of luck in doing so, but I'm going to stick with my decision to terminate the Breakers contract."

"Now, Adrian... Can't we talk about this?" Maxine keeps on with her pleas, but I check out.

Gathering my bag and leaving my dignity behind, I hurry out the door. I want nothing more than to outrun the disappointment I have in myself, but it follows me onto the flight home and wiggles its way inside once I arrive.

I want to be mad at anyone but myself, however, the blame keeps pointing right back to me. First I lay all responsibility on Maxine, but it's still my fault for giving her all the power. Then I blame Roselyn for her spastic behavior lately, but I see reflecting in her the same as in me. It's painfully obvious that we both want out of this charade. She made that clear by skipping the meeting with Adrian.

Unlocking the door and making my way through the dark house, I feel the abyss of solitude pull me under, knowing it's time to put an end to this dark chapter but having no clue on how to conclude it.

Chapter Ten

The bottle and I found our way behind the couch and have camped out all night, but I've kept my lips to myself. Not sure how the bottle feels about that, but I'm close to attacking it as Tuesday evening steals the sun away. I just want to numb the reality of my situation out for a while…

I sit here debating on whether to give in and attack the bottle, weighing the pros and cons. At least drinking doesn't take nearly as much consumption to numb out the pain. It lasts a heck of a lot longer, too. Using food only worked until the last bite, which always had me reaching for a second serving and then a third. The side effects from a sugar high and a bourbon bender are quite similar. Headaches and nasty belly aches.

I don't want to do either. I want to be strong enough to not use any vice as a crutch to get through an episode. I'm stuck in the grips of addiction and don't know how to get loose. I need help, but don't want to allow people to see the darkness.

Feeling hopeless and trapped, I grow thirsty. A key rattles the door as my thumb works the cap loose. It reaches the end of the bottle's threads and pings against the wood floor before rolling underneath the couch. Settling against the makeshift bed of a few pillows and a quilt, I take a fiery sip, thinking Jack will be game in joining me.

"What right do you have skipping my class and then ignoring my phone calls?"

Beck's deep voice startles me, causing the bourbon to slosh down my arm. "You scared me! How'd you get in here?"

"I hunted Jack down." Beck hitches a thumb toward the other side of the couch as a lamp flickers on.

I look up and find Jack peering down at me as he takes a seat on the couch.

"Hey, darlin'."

"Hi." I offer him the bottle, but he declines with a subtle shake of his head.

"The entire class thinks I've killed you off." Beck crosses his arms.

"I'm alive. Sort of… At least Nadine can win the bet."

"What bet?"

"The one where you either murder me or lay claim to me. She bet you'd kill me off."

Jack reaches his hand over the back of the couch and strokes my hair. "Darlin', I've got some business to attend to tonight. You want me to come back afterwards?" His dark eyes look so sad.

And that's my fault, too. I called him while waiting at the airport for my flight and poured my heart out about the weekend and then being fired. I take another sip of bourbon hoping it will help me produce a smile for my concerned friend. I fail at that, too.

I pat his hand. "No. I'll be fine."

"Are you sure?" He glances at Beck and then back to me.

"Yeppers," I say in a singsong voice, sounding nothing like I feel.

After giving me one last look of sympathy, Jack leaves.

"You can go, too. I'm fine." I shoo Beck with a flick of my wrist but he remains rooted in place.

"What's got you hiding this time?"

"Got fired from not only my publisher, but also my agent." That email greeted me this morning. Maxine terminated our contract as well. Good riddance.

"Freelance writers have agents and publishers?"

"No, but a ghost writer does." I take another small sip and offer him the bottle. He takes it but doesn't drink any.

"I'm not following. You're a ghost writer?" He gives the bottle a sniff and grimaces before holding it to his side.

"*Was.* Roselyn got sloppy and screwed it all up." The bourbon is already warming my tongue and this tidbit slips right out.

Beck studies the bookshelf thoughtfully as I ramble on about Roselyn morphing into a spoiled diva.

Glancing over the edge of the couch at the books, I mutter, "We pulled it off for seven bestsellers. Guess that's enough." I wiggle my fingers, beckoning the bottle back, but he opens the French door and tosses it outside. "Why'd you do that for? That was top shelf!"

He ignores my rant and slams the door shut as realization dawns on his handsome face. "You're *the* Roselyn Scott?"

"*No*. I'm Harper Blume, *the* loser not good enough to be the face representing her stories."

"Who's telling you that garbage?" His brows pinch severely.

"My life holds the truth. I've seen it."

Beck shakes his head and steps closer. "Then you're not looking at life clearly."

I have nothing for a comeback, so my lips become mute.

"Let's clear a few things up for you, Blume." He points to the bookshelf. "I've read each one of those books. Now that I know the woman I'm falling for is the author, I'm half-tempted to tie you up somewhere and steal your computer so I can read those stories you've been working on all summer." He crouches down in front of me. "I'm a little embarrassed to admit this, but I actually get a newsletter letting me know about all of the upcoming book releases."

I snicker, not believing what I'm hearing. "You got a thing for Roselyn Scott?"

"No. I've got a thing for your stories." He shakes his head. "You can't possibly think you're a loser."

"Whatever," I deflect with my childish word of choice. I ease off the floor to try for an escape, but Beck catches me by the arm and spins my body to face him.

"Sass and snark won't work this time, so listen up."

Oh great. The drill sergeant has showed up.

"I'm star-struck, but it doesn't surprise me. You are one rare gem."

I try wiggling away from him, but Beck's massive arms lock me against him.

"You're beautiful. Inside where it counts the most, but you got it in spades on the outside."

I stumble over the declaration with my lips working up to smart off, but he moves on.

"Aren't you a southern lady?"

"Well, I'm definitely southern, but the lady part is debatable."

"Either way, I know you've been taught some manners. And this is one you need to get through your gorgeous hard head—you are to say 'thank you' when someone compliments you. It's offensive if you don't."

My mouth remains sealed, thinking he's just saying those pretty words to appease me.

"Harper, take the compliment," he demands, sounding downright mad.

I'm stubborn to a fault and stay silent. Sure, he looks sincere with those turquoise eyes coasting my face in some type of reverence, but I refuse to believe it.

"Stop hiding," he grits out, giving my body a subtle shake. "Let me see you."

I lean away and cross my arms. "I'm right in front

of you."

"You know what I mean… I allowed you to see me and my scars. You owe me and I'm ready to collect."

"I'm not ready to pay up," I blurt, panicking.

His expression hardens. "No room for negotiation."

Before I can rebuke, I find myself slung over his shoulder with him stalking toward my bedroom. Flustered, I slap at his back to no avail.

"Whoa! I'm not ready!"

Ignoring my protest, Beck sets me down in front of the full-length mirror in the corner of the room and brushes off the pile of clothes that curtain it. This reveals a red-faced woman with a menacing man towering behind her. The dire quiet of the room is peppered with our heavy breaths. Mine from being rattled. His from anger, or maybe something else. I'm not sure.

Having my fill of this tense standoff, I go to sidestep but he cages me in with his arms. "Beck," I warn, but he ignores me again.

"Look at yourself," he demands, voice low and raspy.

With no other choice but to obey, I direct my eyes to meet my reflection. Not liking what is before me, I redirect to his reflection and get lost in the deep pools of intense blue locked to mine.

"Such a pale green, those eyes. Never have I seen such a shade before you." His finger traces underneath each eye. "From the first day you glared at me, I've wanted nothing more than to solve the mystery you keep hidden in them." He leans down, heating the shell of my ear with his gravelly words. "I'm getting close."

Not believing his appealing words, my lips pout out to protest and catch his attention.

"And these lips have made my blood boil even before I saw them for the first time. I was tempted several times that week to call you back just to hear you get riled up. Then that morning on the beach, when you pouted out that bottom lip at the end of class to sass, it was all I could do not to lean over and bite it." His thumb traces over my lip before giving it a slight pinch.

I can do nothing but stand still and watch Beck explore me in the mirror. Thankfully, my shirt and yoga pants hide most of me, but I still feel too exposed. His fingertips coast down both sides of my neck. The touch leaves a trail of tingles in its wake.

"This graceful yet strong neck... I don't know whether I want to make out with it or ring it most days."

I glance away from his fingers on my neck to his face in the mirror, finding no playfulness in his expression. Eyes focused and mouth set severely in concentration.

His hands keep moving south, along my sides before rounding to my belly. They come to a rest against my lower abdomen and pull the hem of my shirt up just high enough to expose a strip of pale skin. It's the one spot on my body I loathe the most.

After all of my hard work it still refuses to correct itself. My eyes close to block out the regret.

"Open your eyes, Harper."

I disregard his request and keep them sealed.

"I said open them. Now." There's that ornery authority again.

I finally open them to give Beck a solid glare but soften with finding longing reflecting in his gaze.

Swallowing, I croak, "There's nothing to see here but nasty stretchmarks." I tap his hands.

He suddenly flips his right hand and traps mine underneath, making me touch my skin.

"What do you feel?" His right hand moves mine in sync with his left, causing us both to glide over my belly.

"Ugliness." My answer is immediate and from the severe shake of his head, *wrong.*

Beck ignores me and moves our hands over to the curve of my hips. "Lush, the way a woman should be."

"But it wasn't intended for her to have these ugly grooves marring her skin."

"You're not just any woman, Harper." His fingers trace one of the silvery lines etched along my hipbone once before dropping the hem of my shirt back into place. "This holds testament to your tenacity to overcome obesity. It's a badge of your strength."

"I could gain it all back." Confessing my biggest fear sends a new wave of fear through my body, producing a slight tremble to set in.

He shakes his head again, but accompanies it this

time with a wry smile. "You're too mean to let that happen."

"Maybe so." My chin juts out as I lock my eyes with his through our reflection.

He says nothing, as though he's waiting for something, but I don't know what to give him. The silence stretches with him scrutinizing me and with me wanting to keep hiding from him.

"I fight depression." Another confession comes from out of nowhere. It's like his unwavering search is extracting every one of my insecurities in one fell swoop. I almost add that I've turned to drinking to combat it, but clamp my lips together.

"I know," he whispers. "You don't hide as well as you think you do. I see you, Harper. It's time you see, too."

My eyes begin to sting, so I try sniffing it away, but I'm about to lose the battle. "It's an ugly sight." Tears well and spill, reflecting the shame and disappointment I hold against myself.

"You're seeing yourself all wrong." He releases my hips and wipes the tears away.

"Inner darkness and outer scars... I'm seeing right."

"From that inner darkness comes some wicked creativity." He nudges me to scoot over a bit. "What do you think of me?"

My focus glides down the entire length of him and then back to his somber face. "Perfection," I comment, because he is.

"And my scars?"

"I want to take them on as my own. I want to steal the painful memories caused by them, so they can never hurt you again," I admit, but am stunned that I did.

He lifts a brow in challenge as he hauls me back in front of him and pulls me firmly against his chest. "It's how I feel about yours, but more importantly, that's how God feels. He wants to take away the pain behind your scars."

Suddenly, the ache and pressure becomes overwhelming and sends me gasping for each breath.

"I think I need some fresh air." I step from his grasp and snatch a hoodie from the clothes pile on the floor and shrug it on, needing to cover up what he's made me feel.

Beck quietly leans against the wall. He's said enough, but his body language is speaking volumes.

Not wanting to hear any more, I hurry outside and slump over the deck railing and rest my chin on top of my hands. A long time passes with only the rushing of the tide to focus on. The moon gives off just enough illumination to highlight each wave rolling in. I try timing my breaths with the melody it's making. The sound of the door opening and closing interrupts the progress. I don't turn to acknowledge him, but am soon engulfed in his warmth.

"Will you talk to me about what happened this weekend?" Beck asks as he pulls my back against his chest and hooks an arm around my waist.

I'm relieved he's changing the subject, but not happy with the subject either. "What if I don't want to talk about it?"

The only response is his lips exploring the back of my neck. His teeth take a nip every so often, sending a tingle to shimmy along my spine. I try to squirm out of his hold, but Beck's hands are like vice grips.

"Babe, you need to get still so we can talk right now. Tell me."

Taking a fortifying breath, I begin. "We were to sign with a new publisher this summer. I agreed to pen four more books for the Breakers Series, which seemed like a piece of cake. We've been doing it for seven years now. Me writing them and Roselyn being the front woman. I always send her the first draft so she can study the characters and storyline for the press junkets."

"What happened?" he mumbles before kissing behind my ear.

My shoulder draws up as a shiver seizes me. "For some reason, Roselyn blew off this last book. Not reading it. Not preparing for the junkets. I think the publisher was already suspicious back in June at the last book release party. I should have known right then."

"Your publisher didn't know about the ghost writing deal?"

"No. My agent, Maxine, has always been adamant we keep it a secret. I even had to make Jack sign a confidentiality agreement. She's always paid me through her agency."

"Let's back up for a minute. Explain to me what insane reason it is you're ghost writing in the first place."

"I moved here about ten years ago. Alone. I became a recluse, spent most of my days writing and eating my loneliness away. By the time I had the first three books written, I got antsy to share them. I worked up enough nerve to send out about a dozen query letters and Maxine was the first to respond. Naïve and impatient, I went with her." My voice trails off, not wanting to talk about it.

"And?" he murmurs while massaging my shoulders.

I shrug, not wanting to share the most embarrassing part. I just want to get lost in his touch and do just that until his hand stills.

"Tell me, Harper."

"Maxine wanted me to fly out to New York to sign the contract. By that time, I was at my heaviest and I had stopped leaving the house almost altogether. It became crippling to even make a quick run to the grocery store."

"Harper—"

I brush his hands away and he complies by resting them on my hips. "Maxine flew here and took one look at me… Told me to hold tight, that she had a plan. The rest is history."

Beck tugs at me until I turn to face him. "Where was Jack when all this went down? I thought you two were tight."

I reach over and try smoothing the severe crease on his forehead. "Don't go blaming Jack. He didn't move here until a little more than five years ago. We hadn't seen each other in about a decade before that. And let me tell you one thing, he put his foot down the moment he saw me. Made me start taking care of myself and has been pushing me out of the house with every chance he gets."

"He's fine with your drinking habit?" Beck looks at me skeptically.

"I don't have a drinking habit," I spit out, not liking his accusation. "Jack gets ahold of me if he thinks I'm indulging too much. So no worries there. He's my best friend and always will be."

"What's he say about you ghost writing?"

"That's the only sore spot between us. He's been at me for years now to end it. Says I should have represented my work from the very beginning."

"He's right about that."

I shrug. "Looks like the argument is moot now, considering I'm unemployed."

"You'll figure it out." Leaning down he covers my lips with his and effectively takes my mind off of my career problems, the drinking habit I don't have, and the dark holes I'm unable to fill. Well, he's managing that last part fairly well at the moment…

Beck pulls me over to the lounge chair and reclines it all the way back and points to it before disappearing inside. Before I can settle into the chair, he's back with a quilt and spreads it over me.

It's sweet and tender, but tears spring to my eyes when he climbs in beside me and asks, "Harper, will you please hold me."

This giant of a man with such a big alpha male

ego has just asked me to hold *him*. And I can think of nothing I'd rather do.

*****

This is bad. Very, very bad. Waking up alone has been my norm for the past twenty-eight years, so why does it make my insides pinch this morning? The encounters with Beck keep feeling like dreams that happen in the dark of night and only leave remnants scattering away at sunrise.

Sometime during the dark hours, Beck carried me to bed and left me there even though I asked him not to. He said I was too tempting and it was in the best interest of my virtue he not climb into my bed. It was gentlemanly, but my wayward-self wanted him to not be.

A muffled noise from somewhere in the house draws my attention away from my musings. Smiling, I hop out of bed and make a quick detour to the bathroom to take care of my breath and other needs.

I walk around the corner and freeze in my tracks with finding Beck sitting at one end of the kitchen island in his wrinkled clothes from yesterday while Jack is at the other end in designer jeans and a dark polo. Their rigid body language shouts out a warning for me to turn tail and go back to bed.

Before I can, Beck grouches out, "Is it necessary for him to have a key to your house?" A look of pure irritation paints over his handsome face.

"Is it necessary for him to be spending the night?" Jack fires back before I can answer.

I raise my palms to halt their spitting match. I had no idea Beck even stayed the night. "Yes and yes." I move over to the coffeepot and retrieve a cup before going to take a seat. Thinking better of it, I decide to just lean against the counter instead of taking the stool between these two pouting men. "What's up, Jack?" I ask after my second sip.

He glances at Beck and then back to me, looking uncertain, which is quite an odd look for him. "Just wanted to see how you are after the weekend's crap storm."

There's my eloquent friend. "No worries. I already slipped last night and blew my cover."

Jack's back straightens, looking offended, yet another alien emotion for him. "Oh."

I guess his ego took a blow on this one. It's been only our secret, but now I've gone and shared it with someone outside our little bubble.

"Don't be like that. It's over now and I don't have to keep it a secret any longer." My voice becomes hoarse at the end with remembering my new reality.

He reaches over and entwines his fingers with mine. "Darlin', I know it doesn't feel like it at the moment, but I promise this is for the best."

Beck clears his throat and glares at our interlocked hands.

Jack huffs, gives my hand one last reassuring squeeze before releasing it. "No need in having a hissy fit, man."

Beck ignores him and eyes me. "I was going to make you breakfast, but there's nothing in the fridge besides protein shakes. We need to go grocery shopping."

Dang, he's grouchy, and it's making me antsy to find out what I missed this morning. But I do like how he said "we" in there. Are *we* a couple now?

Jack fires back again with the same amount of vinegar. "That is her breakfast, you schmuck. Seems like that's something you should already know about her."

With anger radiating off his substantial form, Beck stands abruptly, making Jack and I both flinch. Instead of pounding my friend to a pulp, he stalks off to the bedroom, slamming the door with enough force to make the hinges cry out.

"Holy heck! I thought he was about to hand me a butt whooping."

I'm torn between going in there to check on him and staying out here with Jack. I decide to stay put for the moment.

"Do you mind telling me what I missed? Do you deserve a butt whooping?"

He snorts. "He's acting like a little baby because I caught him here."

"Tell me what you said or did to set him off."

He smirks. "Who says I said or did anything?"

I take another sip of coffee, waiting for an answer, because he obviously did.

"I was just joking around, but he ain't got a lick of sense of humor."

"Jackson Calloway, what did you say?"

He shrugs again and takes a sip from his cup. "I only said it'd be hilarious for us both to crawl into your bed and wake you up together. He didn't find it funny."

I reach over and pop him good on the arm. "You're so bad. Not everyone gets your crazy brand of vulgarity."

"I know." He looks over his shoulder. "Seriously, the dude balled his fists and was about to come at me swinging until I apologized."

"I can't believe I slept through all that."

Jack points toward the den, sending my attention through the arched walkway. "You even slept through that, too."

The couch has been moved, so there's no longer an alcove between it and the wall. "When did that happen?"

"After I apologized. Said if I woke you, he'd deliver those fists to my face. I've never moved furniture so quietly before." Jack stands and places his cup in the dishwasher before giving me a hug. "I agree with him. It's time for you to stop hiding."

I silently watch him leave without even replying, and then look at the rearranged furniture. It strikes me hard that these two care enough to call me out on my issues. Blinking back the tears threatening, I go to check on my brooding guest.

As soon as I open the door, a flume of steam floats by me. I hear the shower running.

"Is your girlfriend still here?" He calls out from

the bathroom.

I can't help but smile at his jab. "No. Jack's gone. He sends his apologies if he offended your delicate sensitivities." It was too tempting not to poke back.

The shower cuts off and after a few minutes Beck is standing in front of me, hair dripping wet and with only his pants on. He lifts me to the top of the dresser, making us eye level. "You and I know there's nothing delicate about me."

I nearly swallow my tongue, but manage to say, "I couldn't agree more." I'm not sure I should enjoy being manhandled by him so much, but there's no denying I do. "Where did you sleep last night?"

He hitches a thumb over his damp shoulder. I look over it and find a pillow and blanket on the floor beside my bed. "I didn't want to leave you alone." He leans in and gives me a soft kiss.

"That was delicate." I start to tease, sending him to reclaim my lips in a searing kiss.

Beck draws back suddenly and says, "I'm starving. Let's get dressed and grab some food."

Beck wasn't kidding about starving, only giving me enough time to get dressed and then quickly swinging by his house for him to change into a fresh shirt and jeans. He pulls the Jeep into a diner I've never been to, which is no surprise since I rarely go out to eat.

"Why don't you just grab some stuff to go and I'll sit tight," I suggest.

Beck is already out the driver's door and rounding the back to open mine. "No. I'm starved and need to eat now." He grasps my hand and pulls me out, leaving no room for argument. The man is something serious about his food.

After we're seated in one of the booths with retro vinyl that sparkles and given menus, I feel the anxiety begin to tingle up my spine. The heavy smell of grease and coffee wafts through the place as the chatter of people and the clattering of dishes mingle with the song playing from the corner jukebox.

"Y'all know what ya want?" the bubbly waitress with at least three ink pens sticking out of her auburn hair bun asks.

Beck eyes me. I shake my head, meaning I'm not eating, but he seems to misinterpret. "Can you give us a few?"

"Sure, honey. Can I start y'all with coffee?"

"Sounds good." He offers her a small smile before turning his attention to the menu. "What are you in the mood for?"

"I'm just going to have coffee." I gaze around, taking in the cliché diner décor of the black-and-white checkered floor and neon signs.

"It's almost noon. You need more than just coffee." He slides my discarded menu closer.

"I'll have a protein shake when we get back home. I'm good for now." My stomach betrays me, and lets out a loud, mean growl.

Those aqua eyes look up from the menu. The edge of sternness has them narrowing slightly.

The waitress brings over the cups of coffee and places them on the table, breaking me and the sergeant's staring standoff. "Y'all decided?"

Beck glances back at me. "Any food allergies?"

"Just chocolate. Makes my hips swell," I fire back, thinking that was cute. From the look he's cutting me, the sergeant doesn't agree. Huffing, I answer, "None."

"Any food dislikes?" he asks.

I want to smart off again, but go for honesty. "Celery."

He looks to the waitress and orders, "She'll have the veggie omelet with a side of fresh fruit. And I'll have the same, but could you make mine with three eggs and add a side of whole wheat toast?"

"You got it, honey." She winks over at me, gathers the menus, and heads to the kitchen.

I take a sip of coffee finding it bitter, but drink it anyway.

"Tell me your daily meal plan," he orders before taking a sip from his cup.

I shrug and ramble off, "Protein shake, protein bar, and frozen diet meal. Sometimes Jack will drag me out or bring something over. And I always stick with lean protein and low carb vegetables." I'm proud of this, but Beck doesn't look impressed.

"You're setting yourself up to fail." He stretches his long arm along the back of the booth, the air of casual grace emanating from his imposing form.

How does he pull that off?

Snapping out of my ogling, I ask, "How?"

"From what you've said, you went from binge eating to practically depriving yourself of most foods.

What you're doing now is really no healthier."

I scoff and flick my hand toward him. "What are you, an expert?"

He leans closer, that intimidation he loves to show off back in place. "As a matter of fact, I am. Bachelors in Diet and Nutrition and a Masters in Psychology. I used my sixteen years in the military wisely and got an education."

That was unexpected and firmly shuts down the argument I was working to deliver. No wonder the man is so dang good at manipulation.

The food is delivered and smells heavenly, but the packed diner causes a slight nausea to worry the back of my throat. I expect Beck to dig right in, but he sits and stares at me.

"Eat, Harper."

"I think I'll just have it boxed up for later." I watch the steam rise from the fluffy omelet and try not to breathe its enticing aroma in too deeply. I've tried my darnedest in the last few years to not let food be an enjoyment, viewing it only as fuel needed for my body. The meal I shared with him and now this omelet is making that line blurry.

"Eat it now while it's hot." He unwraps my silverware and places it in my hand.

I set the utensils beside the plate and drink some more of the coffee, instead.

He heaves out a frustrated breath. "Tell me."

My eyes roam around the diner, feeling like I'm being watched. "I don't like to eat in front of crowds."

"Why's that?"

"We've already had this conversation," I snap.

"Look at me," Beck snaps back, drawing my attention away from the crowd. "What others think about you shouldn't matter. Don't let *anyone* have the power over your self-worth."

"I'm not."

"Then hold your stubborn head up high and eat." He points his fork to my plate.

Picking up my fork and slicing a piece of the egg off, I hesitate at putting it into my mouth when I spot a guy looking at me across from our booth. "People are watching me," I mutter under my breath.

Beck scans the diner and catches the guy looking. "The only one staring at you is that guy." He points directly at the stranger, making the guy's eyes scurry back to his stack of pancakes. "He's looking because you are beautiful, and if he doesn't stop I'm gonna kick his teeth in." Beck is still directing the conversation to the stranger, but the man doesn't dare look up from his table.

"Alright, alpha male, calm yourself." I take the bite in hopes of appeasing him enough to leave the guy alone. It's buttery and my taste buds rejoice, but I beg them to go back dormant.

For the remainder of the meal Beck keeps his cool and I manage to eat half of the omelet before giving it to him to finish. He seems to sense that's as good as he's gonna get out of me eating and polishes off the rest.

"What's your plan for the rest of the day?" I ask once we arrive back to the house. I get out, thinking

Beck's going to follow, but he stays seated behind the wheel.

"I have a few personal training sessions later, so I need to get going."

"Oh... Okay." A twinge of disappointment nudges at me.

Beck leans over the passenger seat and drags me back in for a kiss. "See you in the morning. It's the last class, so no skipping and no being late," he says against my lips, kissing me deeply once more before leaning away.

"Yes, sir," I sass before slamming the door and heading inside. The grin on my face is almost painful. His bossiness has grown on me.

The rest of my lonely day passes with me holed up in the office, typing a few chapters, querying a few agents, while ignoring the emptiness I feel without Beck being around. No type of dependence is healthy, so I know I don't need to get attached to him, but that's a whole lot easier said than done.

Chapter Eleven

The sun is high in the sky, allowing a lull in the cool breeze, but my grin remains in place with no lull to that in sight. It's been glued there way past the last boot camp session. I made it through class without running off at the mouth. Beck called me to the front of the group before dismissing us. After the big lug tossed me over his shoulder, he informed the group that even though he'd contemplated my murder at a few points along the way, he decided he'd rather keep me. Poor Nadine had to pay up along with the others who bet on the murdering side of things.

"You look goofy just sitting there smiling like that," Jack says, pulling me from my thoughts. He plops down on the lounge chair beside mine while loosening his tie.

"Where've you been all dressed up?" I ask, eyeing him. Jack normally sports button-downs and dress slacks, but today he's added a tie and jacket.

"Just closed on a new property. We start the renovations next week."

"Another restaurant?"

Stretching out, he places his arms over his head as his eyes droop. "Yes. Italian." He yawns and rubs his eyes with the palms of his hands. "I'm naming it Calloway's Trattoria."

"Dang, Jack, that's impressive."

He mumbles an incoherent response and seems to doze off immediately.

"You've got to stop burning the candle at both ends," I comment, but he doesn't respond. My friend works way too hard.

I remain silent for a while, enjoying the quiet beach from my deck as he softly snores. The rampant tourist season is finally behind us so the day feels pretty tranquil. Thirty or so minutes later, Jack rouses back awake but looks worse for wear, so I brew a pot of fresh coffee.

"Have you heard back from any of the agents yet?" Jack drains the cup and grabs mine from my hands.

I reach over and brush the unruly lock off of his forehead. "No, but Maxine emailed me yesterday."

Jack suddenly looks wide awake. "What did that bat want?"

The lock flops back onto his forehead. He reaches his fingers through it and sends it back into the proper place.

I glance back over the waves before saying, "She's found a publisher who wants to pick up the Breaker's series."

"No, Harper. Not that road again." He grunts, handing my cup back.

"No one else wants me, Jack. I don't feel like I have any other choice."

Jack sits up and faces me, his arms braced on his knees. "Darlin', there's always another choice. Please promise me you'll be patient and wait for it."

"I can't promise that." I worry the hem of my frayed jean shorts, not wanting to meet the disappointment that is surely reflecting from his brown eyes.

"I thought you wanted more. You deserve it."

"Maybe Maxine was right about me being greedy."

"Bull. You're just chickening out because the challenge is too hard."

My gaze snaps up to meet his. "Thanks a lot."

"You know I'm gonna tell you like it is, whether you like it or not."

"And you need to realize this is my choice, and I'll do what I feel is right for my career."

He points at me, glare in place, as he stands up. "I've never been more disappointed in you than I am right now."

"Why are you taking this so personal? It's my life!"

"Because you're cowering out! Grow up, Harper, and live it like a woman. Not a scared little girl, hiding behind any and every thing she can find."

Stunned, all I can do is stay glued to the lounge chair and watch him storm inside. To say that's the harshest Jack has ever been to me is an understatement. Several minutes pass before I hear the front door slam and his car pull away.

"Knock, knock," Nadine says as she steps onto

the deck, startling me.

"Where'd you come from?"

"Nice to see you, too." She takes Jack's spot on the lounge chair. "I met your friend out front. He told me I'd find you back here. Umm... I thought you were with Beck?"

I take the time to look her over. "You clean up good, Nadine. This is the first time I've seen you in something besides workout gear."

She smooths the skirt of her maxi dress while crossing her ankles. "Thanks, but you didn't answer me."

"You distracted me with your pretty hairdo and dress," I tease.

"I already told you I don't kiss girls," she taunts back.

"Jack is a friend I've had since childhood," I finally answer.

"Oh. Well, you keep some stunning company." She whistles low.

I nod my head in agreement. "What's up with you today?"

"My mother-in-law is visiting for a week. Told me to get dressed and get out of the house, so she could spoil her grandbabies in peace."

I chuckle. "So why in the heck are you here?"

She shrugs. "It's the first place that popped in my head after I cranked the van. You wanna go hang out somewhere?"

"What do you have in mind?"

"I'd love to go get a manicure and pedicure."

"But that means strangers will be touching you." My nose wrinkles, causing her to laugh.

"Yes, weirdo. That's a part of it, but the ladies at the salon never bite." She stands and yanks on my arm until I join her. "Come on."

Thinking this will go one of two ways—I could completely freak out or I may actually find the nail grooming pleasant—I decide to take her up on the offer. Either way, it'll get my mind off of letting Jack down.

Turns out, nail grooming isn't so bad. It was sort of pleasant. I couldn't give in to the whole foot washing and massaging idea, but settled for a polishing.

Back in front of my computer, I'm too antsy to write. I need to smooth things over with my best friend. I pick up my phone and text Jack while admiring my fire-engine-red nails.

Me – *I let a stranger touch my toes.*

Jack – *You're into foot fetishes now? Can I watch?*

Me – *Next time. Promise.*

Jack – *I'm holding you to that promise. ;-)*

He sounds like his normal self again, which makes me feel a little better about the decision I'm going to be making soon. Leaving the text message app, I check my emails. The saying *no news is good news* doesn't feel appropriate in this situation. Not one agent has gotten back to me in the last month. Not even a rejection letter has shown up to give me direction. The empty inbox leaves an unsettling void. Wishing to fill it, I text Beck next.

He's off being the real drill sergeant for a week. I miss him, but the time apart has been good for us. We've tiptoed all around the drinking habit he seems to not care for and the worship services I don't care for. I've shown him in the last month I can do without the alcohol by not having one drop. Of that I'm right proud of myself, but the church going has been more painful than breaking up with my beloved bourbon. It always leaves my chest hurting, but the people are friendly and it seems to make Beck happy, so I endure it.

Honestly, Beck makes me happy. Although, it's freaked me out a little with how rapid my feelings have grown for him. When he is around, we can hardly keep our hands off the other. Needless to say, we're acting like teenagers barely holding on to abstinence.

Me – *I let a stranger touch my toes.* I add a photo of my glossy toenails this time to accompany my tease.

Beck – *No one should be touching you but me.*

Me – *Wish you were here touching me.*

Beck – *You can't say stuff like that, woman. I'm stuck babysitting new recruits!*

Me – *But I'm lonely.*

Beck –*Go write a bestseller and behave.*

Grinning at our silly banter, I set the phone to the side and get lost in the new military romance I'm working on. Yes, I said romance.

Chapter Twelve

It's when life is going great and your idiot-self stops paying attention, because you're too wrapped up in your delusional bliss, that something creeps up out of nowhere and attacks.

The cute girl, who showed up at my door this morning, crept into my house offering me a timid smile and kind eyes, blindsided me. The little hussy was a wolf dressed in sheep's clothing and I invited her right on in like a fool.

"Just answer my question. Why have you been hiding behind Roselyn Scott?" the reporter asks for the thousandth time. She dodges around the coffee table as I make a lunge for her. We've been at this game of chase for the better part of an hour with me trying to get the little wolf out of my house and her eluding me.

I chase her through the kitchen before finally getting a grip on her hair. Maybe all that running Beck tortured me with has paid off to an extent.

"You come in here saying you're doing a local survey about beach tourism. That's false pretenses! I'm calling the cops!" I give her a harsh shove toward the foyer when she tries sidestepping me.

"You owe your fans the truth!" She's no bigger

than a minute, but she's definitely got tenacity.

"I owe nothing. Now get out and don't come back here ever again!" I shout while shoving her the rest of the way out the front door. Slamming it and securing the lock, I lean against it and try catching my breath.

Before my nerves have time to settle, another knock hits the door. Thinking it's the little wolf coming back for more, I yank the door open and am blinded by several flashes.

"Miss Blume!" the small crowd of reporters chants out, peppering me with questions of all sorts.

Slamming the door and locking it, I hurry to the French doors to secure those locks as well. Just outside on the sand is another group of cameras. I close the blinds on them and rush to the office to find out what in the heck is going on.

I type Roselyn Scott into the search engine and nearly faint at what pops up.

The Weighty Truth Behind Roselyn Scott...

The Fat Lie of Roselyn Scott...

Roselyn Scott's Hefty Secret...

Each headline is accompanied by a picture that has bile rising up the back of my throat. Not believing it, my eyes scan the shelf where the frame hides. I hurry over and pull it out, wondering how this made it online. The thin coating of dust that usually muddies the image of me at my parents' fortieth wedding anniversary has been recently wiped away. Even though I was well over two hundred pounds, they thought I was an appropriate accessory for that occasion. I stood between them in the picture, wearing a blue evening gown and a forced smile.

Shoving the frame back in its hiding spot, my stomach plummets. Only three people have access to this picture. Beck, Jack, and Nadine. Who would sell me out and why? Nadine is easily eliminated since she's not actually spent much time inside my house, but there's no comfort in leaving the two men I trust the most as the only suspects.

Do you trust me? I got you, okay? Beck's sincerity whispers through my thoughts as tears begin to fall.

Trust me, darlin'. Jack's smooth tone echoes.

Moving back to the computer to shut down the blaring reality, I pause when glimpsing the outlandish number of emails filling my inbox. Hundreds. With no bravery to face it, I shut the computer down and hurry out of the office to get as far away from the hurt as I can. The trek is a short one to the kitchen where a bottle of bourbon sits in wait at the back of the cabinet. It's been there for well over a month, so I pull it out and welcome the amber liquid to do its worst.

Not even two swallows in, a pounding at the front door interrupts my progress of getting sloshed. I ignore it until a familiar voice barks out from the other side. Setting the bottle on the counter, I stomp to the door and slide the security chain in place before cracking it open. As soon as a sliver of Beck comes into view, camera flashes blink behind him.

"Let me in."

"No."

The pucker on his forehead deepens. "Why not?"

"I don't trust you."

He pushes a foot into the door crack before I can get it closed. "I can't help you if you don't explain to me what's going on here." He points a thumb over his shoulder, but I don't dare look at the small crowd.

"Someone ratted me out about the Roselyn Scott situation. It could have been only you, Jack, or Nadine." Tears blur my vision.

"What about your agent or publisher or even Roselyn?"

"You've not seen the picture online?"

Confusion reaches his eyes as they narrow. "What picture?"

"One of me when I was the size of a cow. The very same picture I keep in my office." I release a harsh snort. "How pathetic am I that only three people could be responsible for selling me out. I hope whichever one of you who did it made bank." I push the door aggressively against his foot, but Beck doesn't even flinch.

"I don't know who did this to you, but I'll find out. In the meantime, keep this door locked and stay out of sight," he orders. I wait for him to leave, but he snakes his fingers over to where mine are resting on the side of the door. "I got you, okay?" When I don't respond, he gives my hand a gentle squeeze before stalking off the porch.

The late afternoon dwindles into evening and I can do nothing but sit on my couch, frozen in shock and embarrassment. The phone was the only noise to penetrate the inside of the house until I dismantled it, tossing piece after piece down the garbage disposal and causing another more raucous sound to ring out. But that was hours ago, now only a weird burnt smell lingers from the sink. I ignore it as well as the persistent taps on the door. The politeness of each knock is a clear indicator that another wolf is trying to manipulate me into opening up to them. Already learned that lesson the hard way and there's no desire to repeat the mistake.

The chipping red polish on my toes catches my attention as I rest my feet on top of the coffee table. Only a few weeks back, they were shiny and perfectly done, mirroring how my life felt. The chipping spots and the dulling finish are a strong reminder of how nothing is really ever flawless and one should never trust the illusion of perfection.

A severe knock hits the door, leaving no doubt who's outside. After the third round of pounding, I ease off the couch and go open it, leaving the chain in place. I find Beck and Jack standing on the dark porch.

"Open the door, Harper. Now." Beck's voice is low and raspy and resolutely delivers the order.

I close the door to unlatch the chain, and then reopen it. Before I can get out of the way, Beck shoves Jack inside without entering himself.

"You make this right with her," Beck snaps, giving Jack one final shove, before closing the door behind him.

I glance from the door to Jack as he takes a step toward me. He's disheveled with his hair a mess, shirt rumpled and untucked, but what catches my attention the most is the dried blood around both nostrils and the bouquet of white tulips in his hand. He hands them to me and I accept them in confusion.

Jack has given me these flowers in the past and their meaning dawns on me. White tulips symbolize forgiveness and that is what he wants from me. Understanding hits me so severe the impact sends me to my knees. "How could you?" I screech. "You're my person!"

Jack lands on his knees in front of me, tears streaming down his face. It makes me want to punch him in the face, but from the dried blood and the bruising emerging like a newly developed photo underneath both swelling eyes, I'd say Beck has done enough physical damage there already. Instead, I rear the bouquet back and start whacking him in the shoulder with them, sending confetti of broken petals to rain down around us.

"Shame on you," I gasp with barely enough breath to form words when he remains silent. I whack him one last time with the stems before slinging them across the foyer.

"I am your person. I did it for you." His normally smooth voice presents hoarsely, but I stay firm on not pitying him.

"Thanks a lot! Thanks for humiliating me for *me!*" I scoot away from him so that my twitching fist doesn't lash out. I can't even stand up from the debilitating pain my best friend has inflicted on my soul, so I crawl into the kitchen to where I abandoned the bourbon earlier. I lean up enough to yank it off the counter, plop back onto the floor and take a long pull from the bottle. The liquid fire doesn't immediately take the edge off the hurt, so I take a jagged breath before tipping the bottle back for another go of it.

Jack yanks the bottle away from my lips, sending some of the bourbon to spill down my neck. Using the back of my hand, I wipe it away and slice him a look of pure malice.

"You listen to me…" He pauses to slam the bottle down on the floor and grasp my arms in his trembling hands. "I did do it for you. It's time you own up to who you are, past and present, or you'll never be able to claim the future you deserve. That woman in the picture is just as brilliant as this woman in front of me right now."

I scoff while forming a reply, but Jack gives me a slight shake before I can come up with one.

"Shame on me, Harper?" His bloody nose flares. "No! Shame on you! Shame on you for not loving and respecting the woman in that picture. She deserves nothing less than your absolute devotion and love… Shame on you for making that beautiful mastermind believe she's unworthy…" His voice trails off on a sob and mine joins in.

I push his hands away, not ready to let him close. "But the headlines… the backlash to what you did… it hurts… you hurt me," I stutter between sobs.

"You have to endure it." Jack delivers honesty instead of an apology, staying true to his nature.

I bat the tears away angrily and glare at him. "Why that picture? Why not a recent one?"

"I wanted to make sure you didn't go back to being chained to Maxine. I figured this way you would get the most media exposure."

The epiphany strikes me in a peculiar way. All that time I was heavy, I felt invisible. The hundreds of emails and phone calls and reporters coming at me from all directions today just proved me completely wrong. They saw that heavy woman and responded in an outright frenzy. My shoulders slump and my head bows.

Jack moves over to sit beside me and pulls me close. My first instinct is to push away, but his familiar cologne and the warmth of his touch lures me until my head is resting on his shoulder.

"I still hate you," I whisper.

"No you don't." He presses a kiss to my forehead. "Darlin', I did it with your best interest at heart. Your readers will be able to relate to you better because of it. It'll show you're human with real struggles and not that plastic actress known as Roselyn Scott. I know it doesn't feel like it at the moment, but you're free now to just be Harper Blume."

He reaches over me to retrieve the bottle and takes a long pull from it. He passes it to me as maybe a peace offering. I reluctantly accept it and take a sip and hand it back while taking in everything he just said, but it still hurts no matter his reasoning.

After he takes another generous sip, Jack sits the bottle between his legs and says, "I read this saying once. It goes something like, 'Life isn't about avoiding the bruises. It's about collecting the scars to prove you showed up for it.'" He brushes the hair out of my face and leans slightly down to make eye contact. "Allow the bruises to hurt, but also give them a chance to heal. And be proud of the scars left behind. They prove you not only lived but survived it."

A long time passes with us sitting on the kitchen floor in stillness. Every so often, a hiccup or sob is shared as I struggle to come to terms with the reality Jack has forced me to face. He's right. I could never hate him, but I don't like him much in this moment for making me own up to the shame and self-hate I've been inflicting upon myself for far too long.

✳✳✳✳✳

"If I ever go missing, please put my picture on the back of a bourbon bottle so my person will know to look for me," I slur out while pointing to the empty bottle lying helplessly on its side. Poor thing has been drained dry.

Jack takes a deep breath and nods in agreement. "One thing's for certain, alcohol helps remove many important problems… stress, bras, panties…"

I snicker and slap his wandering hand away from my leg while trying to come up with my next lame joke, but my bleary thoughts are having a hard time producing anything.

Clearing my throat, I whisper with exaggeration,

"Too much of anything is bad for you, but too much bourbon is barely enough."

"Warning," Jack begins with a slurred robotic voice. "Too much alcohol may make you think you're whispering when you're *not*." His eyes go round, cracking me up.

"You are so stupid funny." I snort and snicker.

Jack glances around, blinking several times. "Sergeant Hotshot is liable to tear your kitchen island out if he catches us hiding back here."

We've been rooted to the kitchen floor for what feels like somewhere between a few minutes to a decade, but I have no desire to move.

"We are hidden behind an *island*. He'll never find us." I slice my hand through the air and barely stay upright. We both giggle at that, but was it really funny? I haven't a clue. I look away from the bank of white cabinets in front of us and focus on a fuzzy version of Jack. My finger reaches out and lightly taps his swollen nose. "Can you feel that?"

"A little, but it's pretty numb now. You can kiss it and make it better." He waggles his eyebrows.

"Warning," an angry voice announces, making us both jump out of our skin. Looking up, we find Beck peering down at us from the other side of the island while wearing a menacing scowl. "Too much alcohol is probably gonna lead to you getting your butt kicked again." He lets out a frustrated growl. "This is how you make things right, by getting her drunk? What kind of friend are you? Encouraging her to shove something down her throat, so you don't have to deal with the harsh truth."

"Uh oh. Sergeant Sexy is mad at you, Jack." I snicker.

Jack shrugs his shoulders, tries standing, but falls sideways. It takes him a few attempts to right himself back into a sitting position. "I got it right first. Then we had a little *drunk*." He tries pinching an invisible inch between his thumb and index finger while squinting at it. "It was either bourbon or a chocolate binge. We chose to drink our feelings instead of eating them."

All I can do is roll on the floor, laughing. Jack's so funny... And cute... Even with his black eyes...

"You think I'm cute? Aww!" Jack coos.

I didn't realize that was spoken out loud and this cracks me up until Jack is back to laughing, too. "Like a puppy!" I laugh some more. "Too bad the big bad bulldog whooped ya hiney and messed up your purty face." My hand waves in Beck's direction, but he's not there anymore.

"He only got one punch in," Jack slurs while holding up two fingers, confusing me.

"You're working on some more," Beck warns, appearing by my side on the floor.

"You're magic now? Appearing out of thin air?" I ask, working my fingers to snap but all they'll do is wiggle around like fools. Dang things won't work.

"You feel like eating something or maybe a shower?" Beck asks.

"Shower," Jack and I both answer in unison, sending us back to giggling.

Beck releases a long sigh and scratches at his scruffy cheek. It looks so inviting that I reach out and stroke his other cheek, loving the coarse texture of his stubble.

"You're so sexy," I say before climbing onto his lap and attacking his inviting lips. It takes Beck a second or two before he participates, but he's all in now. Hmm... This man can kiss like nobody's business.

"Let's not do this in front of Jack," Beck says against my lips.

"It's just kissing," I rebuke, but then notice I've yanked his shirt up to his neck. *Oh my.* He moves my hands away and pulls the hem of his shirt back down.

"Don't mind me. I'm enjoying the show."

I look over and see we've captured Jack's full attention.

"Dang, darlin'. Naughty, naughty, naughty." Jack tsks while wagging his finger in mock scolding.

My cheeks flush, but I'm not sure if it's from the alcohol or slight embarrassment. I direct my wobbly focus back to Beck. "I think I've drunk a little too much."

Beck's gorgeous blue eyes roll. "You think?" He taps my thighs before helping me to stand. With an arm braced around my waist to prevent me from slithering back to the floor, Beck looks down at Jack. "I got a good mind to just leave you there."

Jack grins his pretty grin. "I'm fine right here to wait my turn in the shower. Or... we could all fit in the tub at once and conserve water."

Beck props me against the counter and before I know what's happened, he's yanked Jack up off the floor by the collar of his wrinkled dress shirt. "You think you're cute—"

"Harper thinks so, too." Jack grins again and that's when he gets Beck's fist to the mouth. Moaning, Jack cups his mouth with both hands.

"That's just a warning tap. Now get yourself still somewhere and shut it, if you know what's best for you." Beck doesn't wait for a reply, and Jack has wised up enough to not give one.

Before I can chide him for hurting my buddy, Beck cradles me in his arms and moves us to the bathroom. After placing me on my feet, he turns the shower on and adjusts the nobs.

Watching him, I lift my arm and sniff my armpit. "Do you think I stink?"

He turns back to me, his eyes assessing. "Besides the bourbon you seemed to have sprayed on like perfume, no."

"Then why I gotta shower?" I sway a bit, but he grasps my waist to steady me.

"I'm hoping it'll sober you up."

I tsk with a head shake. "Nope. Not gonna work."

"Won't hurt to try." He rubs circles along my back, making me melt against him.

"That's what I thought before that one class of yours. I googled it and that heifer told me it's a waste of time, 'cause only *time* can sober a person." I look up and find a smirk painted on his fine lips.

"Oh yeah?"

"Oh yeah. I tried everything that morning. Long hot shower, a whole pot of coffee... Do you recall it helping me, 'cause I was too drunk to remember?"

I wait for him to tell me I'm right. Instead, he suddenly hoists me up and places me underneath the freezing spray of the shower, soaking my clothes instantly.

Shrieking and hunting an escape, I chatter out, "Cold, cold, cold!"

"Stay," he orders before slamming the shower door shut.

"I'm not a dog!" I yell, cowering in the back corner to avoid the icy pelts.

"No. You're a drunken mess. Wash up." He points to the soap that will put me back into the line of ice water to retrieve it. "Now!" he yells before leaving me alone in the bathroom.

Bracing myself for the frigid attack, I dance over and fiddle with the hot setting until the water warms. I make quick work of stripping off the saturated clothes and washing the booze away. I turn the shower off and dry off. After pulling on a nightshirt, I yank the door open and find Mr. Bossy Pants standing in the way.

Leaning into the curve of my neck, Beck inhales deeply. "Mmm... Now you smell like my Harper again and not a distillery."

The slight sting of his teeth nipping my skin sends a burst of tingles to spread along my body. "I want you to stay with me."

He grunts before stepping back. "Not tonight."

"Why not?" I snap, feeling insecure and maybe a little guilty for showing out. I run my fingers through my wet hair to work the knots loose and maybe some of the tension. "You wanna give me a holy roller lecture on my sin before you run off?"

"No. You're upset. I may not agree with how you're trying to deal with it, but I'll be here to help you through it when you're ready."

"Why? I don't get you!" I throw my hands in the air before letting them slap against my hips.

"Would you rather I belittle you? Ignore your hurt?"

"That's the normal standard for religious folks."

"I'm not into the normal standard." His voice presents hoarsely.

I catch the subtle roll of his throat as he swallows and glances away. I reach out and cradle his cheek in my hand, but he keeps his face turned toward the door.

"I know. I'm sorry for snapping at you... And for putting you through this mess."

His eyes lock back on me. "You need to get a handle on your insecurities. You also need to realize you're the one who is playing judge all the time with slinging up my faith in my face and painting it falsely with the holy-roller jabs." Shrugging my hand away, he starts pacing the room.

Now I feel like a total jerk. "Beck—"

"This is a conversation for when you're sober." He steps over, takes my hand, and leads me over to the bed. "I need to go check on your girlfriend, so please be good and go to bed."

I sprawl out on top of the fluffy blankets and place my arms over my head and pretend we didn't just go so heavy. "Jack won't bother us." I think I even pull off a wink.

"Not happening, babe." Beck tucks me under the covers and heads to the door after a sweet goodnight's kiss.

"Please don't hit him anymore. That's not nice," I say on a yawn while snuggling into the covers.

"I'm not making any promises," he counters before flipping the light switch off.

Alone in the dark, exhaustion begins weighing my body down. As the dizzy day echoes around the room, I give in to it and close my eyes.

Chapter Thirteen

Everything was amusing last night. Fun even. But as light from the midday sun flints through the windows, it shows the glaring truth. Nothing feels amusing now. The darkness of night and the alcohol goggles made it easy to overlook. If the pounding at my temples and this bad case of cotton mouth aren't enough evidence, the scene outside drives the fact home. A horde of intruders are still camped out on the front sidewalk. I shuffle to the French doors and see the beach littered with them as well.

I thought I was caged in by Maxine, but she has nothing on these creepers. I'm about to slink back to bed with hopes of waking up later on the right side of things, but stop when glimpsing a familiar woman pushing a double-stroller through the reporters. She stops by each one and hands them some sort of paper.

"What the…" I croak, stirring a sleeping Jack. He rolls over and slings a leg over the back of the couch and goes back to softly snoring. Shaking my head, I rush to the bedroom to pull on a hoodie and a pair of sunshades.

I rush back to the French doors, crack one open, and hiss out, "*Nadine*." When she doesn't look in my direction, I do it again to no avail.

I helplessly watch on as she hands over a paper to some guy with a giant camera around his neck. She moves to the side of the house, so I storm through the den and on to the foyer with hopes of catching her. Peeping out the blinds, I find her doing the same thing in the front yard.

"What are you up to?" I mutter, while opening the front door a smidgen. *"Nadine."* When she doesn't acknowledge me, I whisper yell, "Nadine!"

She glances in my direction this time, but pushes the stroller over to another group and keeps on her mission. I'm ready to add her to the list!

I chance stepping onto the porch and yell, "Nadine, get your butt in here!" Then, like the coward I am, I run back into the house with my chest heaving in panic. One glimpse between the blinds confirms the barrel of each camera directed to the front porch. I hold my breath until Nadine wrangles the stroller up the steps and to the door. I yank it open long enough for her to hurry in before slamming it and securing every lock. The loud commotion provokes a painful whimper from the den, but I'm feeling a bit spiteful at the moment and can't help but smile with knowing I caused Jack some discomfort. As I've already expressed, I'm not finding things amusing like last night.

Turning to face my other so-called friend, I narrow my eyes at her after shucking the shades and tossing them onto the entrance table. "What the hell-o," I stutter out when I notice two pairs of sparkling eyes peeping up at me from the stroller. Oh wow.

They look like real-life baby dolls with mops of chocolate curls and ruddy cheeks. I blink away the trance they put me under and mutter to their mom, "What do you think you're doing?"

"Beck sent me a picture of you and asked I make this flyer." Nadine offers me one of the soft blue papers.

I brace myself, but let out a sigh of relief when seeing the picture is of me leaning against the rail of the deck a few weeks back. It was at sunset and the evening breeze had my curls dancing around my face while I laughed at something Beck had just said. He was particularly playful that day, and I had no idea he captured the moment in a photo. It was a good moment to capture.

I pull my focus away from the photo in the center of the paper and read the caption.

Harper Blume
Brilliant Beauty Behind
The Breakers Series

"Why would he ask you to do this?"

Nadine hands one of her baby dolls, the oldest, a sippy cup. "I run a small stationary business from home, and he wanted to give the reporters what they're here to get so maybe they'll leave you alone."

"Oh," I mumble, surprised he'd put this much effort in having my back. First he beats up Jack and now this.

"Do you mind if we come in?" Nadine asks while

glancing around the foyer.

"Uhh… Jack is on the couch."

She shrugs her shoulder and points the stroller in that direction. "Okay."

I reach out and stop her. "He's sleeping."

"*Oh.*" A wry smile pulls at the corners of her mouth. "Watch the kiddos for a sec."

"All of my friends are troublemakers," I mumble, knowing *all* only equals two, but what are the odds of winding up with a pair so similar. The things that woman has said over a cup of coffee. I'd almost swear I was talking to a female version of Jack. He met up with us last week and it was quite entertaining to listen to the both of them firing off back and forth. I guess being in the military, a woman has to be able to hold her own, and Nadine certainly knows how.

Shrugging that silliness off, I look down at the toddler and infant. Oddly enough, it's the first time I've met the little cuties. Both are looking up at me, probably waiting for some attention. "You two are so stinking cute."

"Stinking," the little boy repeats like a parrot.

I glance toward the hall and see no sign of their mommy, so I say, "Poop."

His little lips pucker out as he says, "Poop." We both snicker.

Keeping an eye on the hall, I whisper, "Fart."

"Fawt."

Nadine comes around the corner, putting an end to our mimicking game. Her cheeks are rosy and a grin plastered in place. "Can I just go fangirl for a moment?"

"For what?" I ask while bending down to give the infant back the shaky toy she just tossed to the floor.

"You're Roselyn *freaking* Scott."

"Fweaking," the toddler says.

"*Nadine,* you should watch your mouth around impressionable ones." I tsk.

She swats my scold away, not to be deterred. "I can't believe you didn't tell me."

"You own a business you've told me nothing about, so I call us even."

She scoffs. "Hardly."

After we bicker the point for a few more minutes, Nadine takes her little bunch home for their afternoon nap. Feeling inspired by that, I think about crawling back into bed as well. As soon as I step into the den, that idea is forgotten. Jack is sitting up on the couch, hair looking like a rat's nest and face bruised, but what really has me looking twice is the thick black ink scribbled along his forehead that says HIT ME.

Snickering and then snorting until full-out laughing, I step a little closer to take in Nadine's handy work.

Jack cringes and covers his ears. "Stop making all that racket." He groans when I plop down beside him, making the couch jostle.

"Serves you right."

"I know," he croaks. "I'm sorry for not being a better friend."

I glance at him. "Yeah. What you did was pretty sorry."

"No. Not the picture. The drinking."

"Oh," I groan. "Don't get all spiritual on me."

He scrubs his hands over his face, but winces when he reaches his nose. "You know I see no harm in having a drink or a slice of cake, but that's where I've been a bad friend... Harper, you can't stop with just one."

My throat thickens and a wave of nausea joins in my discomfort. "I know."

Jack reaches over and takes my hand. "I think it's time we stop this mess. It's only making us a *hot* mess."

Tears trek down my face as I nod in agreement. "You have no idea how much of a hot mess you are at the moment." I let out a watery laugh.

"Ugh. I know." He gingerly touches his nose and then his cheeks. "It'll fade in a few days."

"Yeah, 'cause I have a feeling it won't wash off." My eyes land on the permanent marker sitting on the coffee table.

Jack looks at me curiously before standing and stumbling into the bathroom. Moments later, the sound of him groaning sends me back to laughing.

*****

"You're going to have to face your inbox sooner than later." Jack looks up from my laptop where he has it perched on his lap.

I look away and watch as an elderly man walks

by with his dog. The tiny yapping beast keeps snarling at the encroaching waves before he scurries back to his owner. Only a few other people have wandered out to stroll along the gloomy shore today.

Luckily, the beach is back to its fall dormancy after the long week of disorder from the paparazzi has finally died down. Some celebrity couple who became a couple after being caught in an affair has now split because the guy was caught cheating. Karma can be a biddy if you don't play nice. Thankfully, their bad karma has taken the attention off of me and has sent the cameras scurrying away like the rabid stalkers they are.

"Hello?" Jack snaps his fingers.

"I know." I hitch my shoulder with a little attitude. He and Beck both have been pushing me to come out of hiding.

"Stop being so darn stubborn." He shoves the laptop in my lap. "I've weeded out all of the trash and made two folders. One is filled with agents asking to represent you and the other is fan mail."

"Thank you," I mumble while eyeing the folders underneath the inbox tab.

Jack stands and stretches his arms over his head, releasing a long groan. "Took me long enough. I've gotta go button down a few things before flying out next week."

I glance up. "Where are you off to now?"

"To my parents. They've been at me to go visit."

"Such the good son." I roll my eyes.

Secretly, I'm jealous of how close Jack's family is,

wishing mine were the same. I'm even jealous of Beck's family. They are the same way. My dad did take the time to call, via Jack's phone since I've not replaced mine, when they got wind of the Roselyn Scott debacle, but only to reprimand me from keeping such a secret from them. It was all about how my mom was so upset she couldn't even leave the house, and how Dad felt so disrespected by his only child. Nowhere in that phone call did he ask how I was doing or offer not so much as one word of encouragement.

"Do me a favor," Jack says, glancing at the waves then back to me while rubbing the back of his neck.

"What's that?"

"Stop holding back from Beck."

"What do you mean?" I close the lid to the computer and stand up from the lounge chair.

"Ever since the photo came out, you've been avoiding him. Why?" He motions for me to follow him inside.

"I'm embarrassed." I shrug. "He not only saw me in that picture, but I'm pretty sure I made a fool of myself that drunken night." Grainy images of me throwing myself at him and him turning me down flicker through my mind, making me wince. Then there's the fuzzy part where he called me out on making fun of his faith. That makes my stomach hurt in shame. I rub it, wishing to soothe my stupidity away.

Jack snorts. "From what he said to me after you passed out, I'd say he didn't mind it."

I stop in my tracks while the heat blooms across my cheeks. "Shut up. What did he say?"

"Well, he started off by threatening to cut my manhood off if I ever did anything to hurt you again. Then he went on to say that he wasn't going anywhere and I'd better learn my place in you two's relationship. Whatever in the heck he meant by that."

A snicker slips from my lips. "He thinks you flirt too much."

"See." Jack's eyes go round. "The man wants you. Stop being a pansy." He waves toward the door. "Might I suggest you invite him over and greet him at the door in a short tight dress?"

"Jack!" I pop his arm.

"You owe him at least that much for putting up with you." He grabs my hand when I go to deliver another pop. "Seriously, he's crazy about you and it wouldn't hurt for you to show him how much you care, too, while you're *sober*." All of the tease is gone from his brown eyes and only sincerity reflects from them now. As he opens the front door, Jack leans over and places a kiss on my cheek, but then yelps.

I look up and find Beck standing in the open doorway. "You forget our talk so easily?" He glares at Jack.

"Perfect timing, hotshot. I was just trying to talk Harper into inviting you over. You're welcome." Jack returns the glare while rubbing his upper arm. Looks like Beck's hits are more lethal than mine.

"No spitting contest today, boys," I scold while taking a step between them.

"I'm out. See you soon, darlin'." Jack bravely gives me a hug, but Beck keeps his fists to himself this time. Then Jack does something I didn't think he was stupid enough to do. As he passes by Beck, he shoves into his shoulder, body checking him with enough attitude to start a war.

I brace myself for the repercussions, but Beck only shoves back into him and slams the door before Jack is completely out of the way.

"Y'all are something else... It's making me question if you're hiding a bromance," I tease.

He completely ignores my taunting and says, "Let's go grab a bite to eat."

Trepidation claws at my shoulders from the thought of leaving the house. Sure, he managed to push me out the door a few times to eat or shop for more substantial groceries before last week, but I feel like I'm back to square one.

"I'm not hungry." I go to move past him, but his arm drapes over my shoulder and spins me back around.

"It's going on suppertime. Let's go." Beck veers us to the door and doesn't let go of me until I'm strapped into the Jeep's passenger seat.

He pulls out of my driveway and in no time is pulling into his. I look over at him in question, but he remains silent until we are inside his house. I've only been here a few times. Unlike my pudgy one-story cottage that is nestled in the sand, Beck's beach house is two-story and on stilts across the road from the beach. Another contrast is where my place is light and airy from its shabby chic style, Beck's is all dark and masculine with teak wood and leather furniture.

But it's different tonight. A softer vibe lures me to the flickering light of candles dancing around the dim dining room. The table is dressed with dishes and flowers.

"Wow, Beck…" I glance at him as he walks us to the table. "I didn't know you had this in you." I motion to the romantic scene.

"I figured I had to step up my game since you seemed to be growing bored with me." He pulls a chair out and helps me have a seat. And what I love the most is he takes the chair right beside me and not the one across from me.

"I could never grow bored with you," I whisper while searching the table. A vase filled with delicate peonies sits in the center and is surrounded by the candles. "Those flowers are beautiful."

Beck grunts. "Took me forever to find ones that smell like you. Those are pretty close. I think the florist thought I was nuts, going around sniffing every bin of flowers she had." He glances at me from the corner of his eyes as he scoops salad onto our plates.

All I can do is look at him in awe. "Why would you go through so much trouble?"

"You're worth any trouble, Harper." One side of his lips curls up while he busies himself with preparing our plates. He hands me a glass of iced water and taps his against it before taking a sip. "Tell me why suddenly you don't seem interested."

When he remains quiet waiting for an answer, I produce one. "I figured you were probably over your interest in me, so I was giving you a clean out."

Beck hands me a fork and points to the salad, bossing me as always. "What gave you that idea?" He takes a bite and chews thoughtfully while watching me.

I follow suit to buy some time. Swallowing, I finally mutter, "I'm not sure if you've seen that picture—"

"The one Jack shared?" he asks and I nod. "Yeah, I saw it. So?"

"Well, between that and me behaving like a drunken idiot, I assumed that was enough to have you running in the other direction."

Beck shakes his head while removing the lid from a serving dish, releasing a robust aroma of garlic and herbs. Nestled inside is roasted chicken and vegetables. It smells amazing but my stomach is flip-flopping around, making it doubtful I'll enjoy the meal. While he adds some roasted vegetables and a slice of chicken breast to my plate, I take another gulp of water.

We eat in amicable silence until most of his plate is empty and mine barely touched.

"Will you do something for me?" he asks, offering me a bite from his fork. I accept and nod. "Until you figure out how to face your life, will you lay off of the heavier drinking?"

"You're one of those who think all the mentions in the Bible about wine are really grape juice?" I raise both my eyebrows for emphasis since I can't figure out how to send only one into a high arch.

"I'm not going to sit here and debate Biblical interpretations with you. I personally see nothing wrong with having a drink in celebration or to accompany a meal, but it's not okay for you to shoot back an entire bottle of alcohol to drink away whatever it is that's bothering you." Beck hitches a foot in the leg of my chair and yanks it so I'm facing him. He braces his hands on the back of it to cage me in. "You can keep filling the voids with food or snark or expensive booze all you want, but until you mend the cause of the holes, the pain is going to keep pouring out."

His statement stills my squirming. All I can do is sit with my gaze locked on his beautiful, sincere eyes. He moves one hand to cup my cheek.

"I'm scared," I confess.

"Of what?" he asks in a softer tone.

My heart kicks up in beats. "Of rejection, failure, of not being good enough."

"So instead of acknowledging the life just begging for your attention, you choose to hide from it like a coward." He doesn't form it into a question, and before I can snap at him, he plows on. "Besides, you're too stubborn to let any of that happen."

I scoff and roll my eyes.

"I've got proof," he retorts. "You put yourself out there to snag up that first agent. You shared your stories, knowing failure could happen. You've proved seven times to the world you're more than good enough with your writing skills."

I glance down, but Beck places a finger under my chin and gently tips it so that my focus is back on him.

"But those are only examples of your creative talent... Harper, so much of your life is unwritten, because you allow fear to hold you back."

"I don't understand why you even care."

"Your life matters to me but let me show you where it really matters."

I haven't a clue what Beck means by this until he loads us up in the Jeep and drives us down the coastline and back to the familiar beach access lot.

He leans over the seat and places a tender kiss on my lips. "This is where it matters the most. Please just give it a chance."

We walk hand in hand across the street and over to the pavilion that is alight with strings of lights and people singing. Oddly, it feels like we are walking up to a beach party and not a worship service. A band is set up at the front of the group and is belting out a lively song about singing of His love forever. People have their hands raised in the air and are dancing along to the beat the instruments are creating.

"This is weird," I mutter to Beck and try pulling him to a halt.

He doesn't allow me. Instead, he swings me around and starts leading us in a dance. "It's only weird because you don't understand it yet."

"Aren't Christians supposed to look differently from the world? This place looks like a frat party minus the kegs." I look around and see only euphoric smiles gracing everyone's faces.

"Exactly. No kegs needed. We're high on joy. *That* is different from the world. If we hide our joy, then we rob the world of seeing what they're missing out on."

I keep a hold on my confusion, using it as a shield to suppress those peculiar feelings from building in my chest for a few songs, but it slips when my focus shifts from the rhythm of the music to the words being sung.

Live like you're loved. You're valuable. God loves you just as you are. Be who He made you to be. He holds your soul, so don't be afraid to live in that grace. No more guilt… No more shame…

The intensity grows in my chest until I'm gasping for breaths.

"I'm having chest pains." I rub at my chest, desperate for relief.

"It's not chest pains. It's soul pains."

Tears burn my eyes. "How to make it stop?"

Beck turns so that I'm shielded from the group by his large form. "Easy. Just give your life over to God. Ask Him to heal those holes in your soul."

I shake my head and press my palm firmer against my chest. "I don't know if I can give my life over."

"Harper, it'll be the most freeing experience of your life. You've not truly lived until you do this." He leans down and fixes his lips near my ear and whispers, "Ask Him to heal the holes."

I want nothing more than to fix whatever is broken in my chest, so I do. As soon as I stop rebelling against it, the most peculiar thing happens. My soul shatters, releasing all of the darkness that has been trapped inside for far too long. The sultry night feels heavy with all of the jagged pieces suspended in it, some float away while others seem to strengthen. Beck keeps his lips pressed to my ear and leads me in a prayer and by the time he concludes both of our faces are damp with tears. This moment feels like a fairytale and I wouldn't believe in it had I not been living it. I truly feel the holes mending as the pieces of my soul weave back together. The tapestry of my being may never be complete in this lifetime, but I know it's a pattern I'll be more comfortable wearing.

I can't help but giggle from feeling so light all of a sudden, like the burden evaporated right along with my tears.

"It only gets better."

"You say that about a lot of things."

"No. I say that about only one thing."

"What's that?"

"Life, and, babe, it will only get better." Beck grins down at me and continues dancing us in a celebratory circle.

I can't help but muse over how I've allowed ridiculous religious rituals that don't matter a hill of beans to rob me of a joy just waiting for me to claim. All those years trying to live up to some impossible standard put into place by men and not by God. Their man-made malarkey was to keep a bridle firmly set in the members' mouths. I allowed it to be my reason, no, my excuse to not write the life God had intended for me to live and to rebel like a brat. Beck has shown me I don't have to be anyone but Harper Blume. Him showing me this side of God's people has also shown me I can come as I am and not what people expect me to be. It's truly the most freeing epiphany of my life.

Once the service concludes, Beck walks us across the street, bypassing the Jeep, and on to the beach. We kick our shoes off and continue dancing.

"Tell me a story. Our story," he eventually requests.

"I've lived a life void of desire until glimpsing a picture of you. That first desire was born from curiosity and longing for something I didn't understand…" Words fail me as the emotions thicken my throat.

He leans away from me abruptly. "Tell me more."

I open my eyes and find those blue depths of his gaze locked on me.

It takes a few moments to get back to the story and when I do, my voice is unrecognizable. It's low and husky. "Another aspect of desire met me on the beach that day. Never have I wanted to slap someone and kiss them at the same time until I met you."

We both chuckle.

Taking a few deep breaths, I continue with my lips admitting a truth my mind had yet to comprehend until it's articulated. "Desire is faceted on so many levels. I didn't grasp that until you. Never have I felt worthy enough to expect anything from this life until now. You've ignited a desire in me to want it all. But my greatest desire is to love you *through* all of it."

Beck blinks several times. "You love me?"

The affection reflecting from his handsome face and the sweet smile gracing his lips compels me to confess how I truly feel about him. Cupping my hands to his face, tears tickling the corners of my eyes, I whisper, "I'm in love with you. I promise I tried not to, but—"

"I love you, too, Harper."

Overwhelmed by this declaration, my eyes close to help savor it.

"Open your eyes and live in this moment with me," Beck quietly demands.

I do as he says and regain a bit of control. With eyes locked on mine, he leans down slightly to brush a kiss onto my parted lips. We breathe the air the other offers with our bodies swaying in time with the ocean's luring melody.

"I love you, Harper," Beck says resolutely, bringing me back to him as he rests his forehead against mine.

Beck's words from earlier penetrate the blissful fog. *Babe, it will only get better.* His declaration was an understatement. It's complete rapture.

"Beck, thank you for accepting all of my brokenness and for not giving up until I allowed God to put me back together."

He releases a long sigh and rasps out, "You own me."

There's no doubt he owns me, too.

Chapter Fourteen

Sunlight filters through the checkered curtains as my thoughts continue to remain on last night. Stretching, I feel the ache in my calves and can't help but grin from its presence. We danced the entire night away and are now sitting in the diner scarfing down breakfast.

"What are you smiling about?" Sleep rumbles Beck's deep voice.

I look over and see him watching me with his head tilted to the side as he takes a bite of bacon.

"You know why. I'm feeling so light and free, I could float away."

He reaches over and presses his hand on top of mine. "But I like you here. No floating away, Blume."

I grin and blink my heavy lids. "I like being here with you too much to float away just yet."

"I like that smile you're wearing. It's genuine." Beck leans over the table to steal a quick kiss. "You wear it well," he whispers against my lips before sitting back.

My lips stretch even wider from his compliment as my fingers touch the delicate petals of the peony tucked behind my ear. Beck swung by his place to grab the flowers so I can take them home. He kissed me in his driveway and then tucked a smaller bloom into my tangled hair, saying the flower was the perfect symbol for me. I was flattered that he took the time to look up the meaning of the pink peony. It symbolizes healing, and I feel my soul doing just that.

"It's a feeling like no other, isn't it?" Beck asks, somehow reading my thoughts.

"Yes. It's euphoric."

He takes a sip of coffee. Once the cup is back on the table, his eyes have taken on a serious note. "Just remember when a difficult chapter comes up—'cause, babe, it will—hold on to this epic moment." He entwines our fingers. "Remember, nothing worldly can take care of it. Turn to God."

The food binges and drunken nights flash before me. Each time I turned in either direction, I was always left in worse shape than I began. There's no way I want to go back to that, but naivety could easily sway me to turn there. Beck is right to remind me. Here's praying my life story can stay on the right track.

Tears tickle my eyes as I nod with understanding. Sniffing them back, I take my last bite of egg and wash it down with some coffee.

"We've got to go to bed soon. I'm about to fall into my plate of food," I say on a yawn.

"Sleep will have to wait for me. I've got training sessions to get in first, but I'd like to take a nap on your deck later on."

"Sounds like a plan to me." We grin at each other like goofy kids, but I don't care. I'm too happy to care.

After finishing up breakfast, we head back to my cottage and find a new Prius parked in my driveway. For such a froufrou car, somehow this one with dark tinted windows and a gunmetal paintjob pulls off an edgy look. Beck parks beside it and is rounding the Jeep before I know what's happening. I grab the vase of flowers and scoot out of the seat.

A man emerges from the car with his hands held up in surrender.

"Harper, you know this man?" Beck's gruff voice and glare is enough to have me a bit nervous.

I glance at the man in question with his salt-and-pepper hair, bowtie, and thick glasses. His eyes are trained on the impending attack while his head nods.

"Yes, he's Adrian Wild. My publisher... or was going to be until—"

"You're the one who fired her?" Beck takes another step until he's leering over Adrian with clenched fists.

I reach up and brace Beck's shoulder. "It's okay. Adrian had every right."

He ignores my attempt to calm the situation. "Do you realize how talented this woman is?"

Adrian adjusts his glasses and steals a quick glance at me before regarding the giant threat in front of him. "Yes. That's why I'm here to right my wrong."

Beck jabs a finger just shy of Adrian's chest, making me flinch right along with Adrian. "You better." He takes a step back and pulls me to him, effectively blocking me from Adrian. "I've got to get to those training sessions, but I'll be back as soon as

I'm done."

"Okay," I mumble just before he kisses me. It's tender and delicate and amazes me that just seconds ago he was all menacing.

"I love you," he whispers against my lips.

"Love you, too."

Releasing me, Beck conveys another warning glare to Adrian before climbing inside the Jeep and leaving me to deal with whatever this may be. We both stand in the driveway, a bit stunned, until the Jeep rounds the corner.

"Now that is a noteworthy book boyfriend," Adrian admits, his tone full of respect.

Snickering, I turn toward him and ask, "Now what would you know about book boyfriends?"

His lips pull into a smirk, showing off distinguished laugh lines. "I own a publishing house. It's my job to know what sells." He points to where the Jeep just disappeared. "And that, young lady, *sells*."

"I've definitely bought into it."

"Are you incapable of replying to an email or answering your phone?" he asks abruptly, sounding rather fatherly.

"Umm… My computer and I broke up and my phone blew up." With my defenses going up, the snark joins the fight.

"You have one of those phones making headlines with the battery catching fire?"

"No. I have a garbage disposal that's addicted to cell phones."

Adrian lets out one of those nasally laughs and shakes his head. "Now there's the Harper Blume I met that night at the release party. So glad to see you again. May I come in?" Adrian asks, making me aware of how rude I'm being.

"Oh, sorry. Sure." I lead us inside and on to the kitchen, place the flowers on the counter, and stealing a long sniff of their sweet perfume before turning back to Adrian. "Coffee?"

"Yes, please." He settles onto a stool, places a briefcase on top of the one beside him, and folds his hands. "I must say, Miss Blume, you look much different than the last time I saw you."

My cheeks warm, wondering if last night's revelation is advertising as brightly as a neon billboard sign. I keep my back to him until the coffee maker sputters to life. Pulling on an air of bravery, I retort, "Last time you had just squashed my career."

"Nonsense. I did you a favor." There's a sharp edge of irritation in his tone, making me whip around to eye him. As soon as our eyes meet, he says, "I'm quite disappointed in you."

"Me?"

"Yes. I waited for you to stand up for yourself. Instead, you acted like a coward and ran out of my office."

I'm tired of being called a coward. Every irritating man in my life has chosen to voice this in only a span of one week. Tears sting my eyes. I sniff them back and look away.

Adrian places his hand on top of mine and lightly

squeezes. It feels fatherly and makes me homesick for something I've never had. "I thought I found an individual cut from the same cloth as myself when we met. One who wanted to be unique, instead of blending into the generic fabric society likes to weave everyone in until there's no distinction left. You're too brilliant to blend, my dear one, and it's past time you stand up and stand out."

While pondering his words, I turn around and busy myself with pouring us a cup of coffee. Funny how he used fabric for his object lesson, because lately I've viewed my life as threads, weaving in a different pattern. One that finally feels to be a proper fit.

"Adrian, why are you here?" I place a cup before him.

After taking a sip, he places the cup back down and answers, "I'm here to save you from the sharks."

"What sharks?"

"The agencies trying to get their claws into you. You have to know this."

I shake my head. "I've sort of been in hiding since that picture."

"Everyone's scrambling to figure out how to snag you up. I'm surprised I'm the first to show up on your doorsteps."

"I'm not so sure you're the only one." I rub my palms against my temples. "There have been plenty of visitors, but I assumed they were all paparazzi so I've not answered the door."

"Smart move." He reaches over and fishes out a folder from the briefcase and hands it to me. "This is what I'm here to propose."

I flip through the papers, finding a contract and a seven-figure check made out in my name. Gasping, I look over at him and hold up the check. "What?"

"Wild Idea Publishing has wanted you from the start. *You*, Harper Blume. Not an actress named Roselyn Scott. That folder was sitting on my desk during our meeting, waiting for you to demand your rightful place. Instead, you ran."

"I'm sorry."

"Why are you apologizing?" His voice fills with trepidation.

"I'm sorry for being a coward that day. For being a coward for most of my life, for that matter."

"You're twenty-eight, correct?" The edges of his eyes soften, conveying that fatherly vibe once again.

"Yes, sir."

"Young lady, I think you can get a pass this once. Live and learn, and then live some more. Yeah?"

"Yeah." There's no containing the grateful smile pulling at my lips. Adrian Wild is the first person to tell me it was okay. To give me a pass for my mistakes. I really like this peculiar man.

He pulls a card from the pocket of his lime-green button-down and slides it across the counter top. "This is my personal number and I've written the number of the hotel I'm staying at here in town. Have your lawyer look over the contract and get back with me."

Studying the card, I ask, "How long are you here?"

Adrian taps the contract. "Until you sign this." His eyes crinkle as he offers a kind smile, a smile promising me every career dream I've ever wanted. "With everything coming out in the last week, I'd also have your lawyer look into your options with the Roselyn Scott books."

"Okay." I gather everything into the folder with slightly shaky hands. It feels like I'm dreaming right now.

After he drains the cup, Adrian stands and reaches for his briefcase. "And, Miss Blume, also get a new cell phone and keep it away from the garbage disposal."

Adrian Wild offers a reassuring pat on my shoulder before leaving me with a lot to think about.

*****

"Hello?" Adrian's voice muffles through the phone.

"This is Harper. I bought a phone." I stare at the door in front of me, stunned that I've spent my entire day actually out and about in public.

Surprisingly, no one cracked a fat joke nor did they act judgmental. It made me realize that, yes there will be critics, but Jack was right all along. I'm being more accepted than shunned, and that's why I finally feel worthy enough to stand at this door and claim my identity.

"That was quick."

It only took two days to get everything in order to finalize this next chapter. Never have I been so ready to begin one in all my life.

"Yes, and if you could open this door, we can quickly wrap up some business." I raise my hand to knock, but the door opens before I manage it.

Dressed in a grey button-down with a pink plaid bowtie and dark-wash jeans, Adrian motions me inside the hotel suite. It's ultra-modern, reminding me of his swanky office. "Are you sure you had enough time to go over the contract?"

"Yes, I just left my lawyer's office." I sit on the couch he directs me to and hand him the folder.

"You understand I want exclusive publishing rights? No middle man?"

"Yes. I will work directly with you. I really like that idea." I smile while smoothing my skirt. I feel like a grownup today for the first time. Fixed my hair and everything.

"Good, good. I say we go out and celebrate."

My smile falters but then picks back up when I dare the coward lurking inside to whine about it. I've given that part of me too much power for way too long. "Sure."

"Okay. This is your town so I'll let you lead the way."

"I'm a recovering recluse, so we are both in the same boat." I think for a moment and pull my phone out. "But I may have a *wild* idea." I wink at him while dialing Jack's number.

*****

I reach over and slap Jack on the arm with as much strength as I can muster up as soon as he sits down beside me.

"Ow!" He rubs the offended spot while slicing me a look. It's equal to my own scowl. "What was that for?"

"A male review? Really? This is what you come up with when I ask for a night out!" I yell over the pulsating music. My eyes flicker back to the stage that's tucked on the third floor of Vel. A private floor where at the moment is displaying lots of male perfection. The performers sway to the hypnotic music while the flashing stage lights follow them around the slightly raised platform. Thank goodness, they are keeping most of their clothes on. Only losing their shirts during the dance routines. I tear my attention away and look back at my mischievous friend for an answer.

"This was already scheduled and I had to be here. Thought you'd get a kick out of it, beings you've only recently been introduced to the male species. Wanted to make sure you understand there are plenty of options." Jack's grin is rascally until his face transforms into a grimace. "Dang it! Y'all gonna leave bruises." He rubs his other arm while glaring over at Beck.

"Move!" Beck yells while shoving Jack to make room for himself beside me on the long couch. He leans close and whispers loudly in my ear. "Looks like your new boss is having a good time."

We both crack up while looking over at Adrian Wild where he stands close to the stage, an older woman on each arm. One has procured his bowtie and is now wearing it around her neck.

I take another sip of water, not needing the effect of alcohol. The scene before me is dizzying enough. I lean over and yell, "He's probably second-guessing my contract now."

"Nah. There's no sign of a regretful man over there."

"Nadine's husband is looking a little regretful, though." I tip my bottle of water in their direction, watching my giddy friend jump up and down while gripping her husband's arm.

"I bet old Mick won't mind later on tonight when he gets his worked-up wife home."

Luckily, Nadine's mom took her two children overnight. She and her husband were just as stunned as I was when we entered this room with its wild show. Nadine warmed up as fast as Adrian, but it's taken the rest of us aback.

"Seriously, Jack. What's the deal with this?" I yell into his ear.

He points to the considerably large group of elderly ladies cheering at the edge of the stage. "It's their fault. They hoodooed me. Said this was a fashion show fundraiser... *For the children*, of course."

"Of course." I burst out laughing and watch a few of the ladies high-five each other. "I've never seen such a fashion show as this one before."

"You won't see it here again either. Mrs. Gertie and I had a heart-to heart talk, and I told her she wouldn't be pulling a stunt like this over on me again." Jack shakes his head, looking a little put off by having someone getting something over on him.

The show continues raining men for the next longest stretch of time. A fireman sets the place ablaze. A policeman instigates pure mayhem instead of bringing order to the place. And a distinguished businessman in a black suit and grey tie struts around the stage. There's no doubting the grey-haired ladies paid a fine penny to book this show. Each act is well choreographed and the men are clearly professionals.

By the time we leave Adrian in Jack's care—no, that's probably not a good idea—my ears are ringing and my mind is reeling.

"What was your favorite model?" Beck asks as he steers the Jeep onto our beach road, the nightlights welcoming us back home.

"I don't know… Maybe the cowboy. Sorta inspired me to want to take up riding."

Beck growls and shakes his head.

I cluck my tongue. "To be honest, I'm quite disappointed."

"Why's that?"

"There wasn't one military guest. Now that would have been *hawt*." I giggle when he cuts me a menacing look.

Once parked, Beck walks me to the door, but doesn't make a move to go inside.

"Don't you want to come in?" *Please!*

"Not tonight, babe. I think you've had enough excitement for one evening." He runs his fingers through my hair and leans down to give me a chaste kiss. "Good night."

"Stay." I reach out and try stopping him, but he's stronger and makes it down the porch steps.

"Another night. Go to bed and behave."

"You know how I feel about behaving."

"Don't make me bend you over my knee and spank you," he says sternly.

"I kinda like the sound of that," I call out, hoping he'll turn around and chase me inside.

He doesn't turn back to scold me, just loads up and drives away. Disappointed, I head inside and lock the door. The clock reads close to one in the morning, but I'm wide awake and a little frustrated by Beck's attitude. Guess I wouldn't be too thrilled spending the evening with him watching women strutting around, so I let it go and make my way into the bathroom to shower off the night's shenanigans.

Once that's done, I slip into a nightshirt and head to the kitchen for a bottle of water. Just as I take a sip someone knocks on the door. I hurry over to peep out the blind and see the Jeep is back. Excited, I sling the door open but freeze with dread at the sight of him.

No!

"Please tell me you don't have to go," I barely squeak out while taking in Beck's Army fatigues. Head to toe in camouflage and black combat boots strapped to his feet. His hat is pushed low over his eyes, but those full lips are on display and pressed in a severe line.

"I'm a soldier, Blume, and a soldier has to follow orders. No matter what."

The lump in my throat won't allow me to swallow and tears instantly blur my eyes.

"Please don't—"

"No room for negotiation. My orders tonight are to give you a thorough inspection." His lips twitch before he lunges at me. I'm slung over his shoulder before I can comprehend his words.

"You jerk! I thought you were leaving me for an assignment." I slap at his back as he walks me to the living room.

"Ma'am, you wanted a soldier, and I'm here to deliver." His voice is full of command and makes me shiver all over. He pops my behind rather harshly before planting me in the wingback chair.

The sexy soldier docks his phone into my speaker port and cranks up "Sexyback." He found out I use that for his ringtone, so I guess it's the perfect song for this unexpected performance.

"Oh… Hawt!" I squeal, watching him whirl around as his imposing body starts moving to the song. This model of male perfection fills the space with his presence and makes me pure dizzy.

And he's still completely dressed!

Whistling and catcalling, I watch those lean hips of his undulate to the beat as he begins working the buttons free on his jacket. The garment makes one rotation over his head before landing across the room.

Beck's massive hands move over his tight T-shirt, gripping the front, and then, *holy moly*, he rips that sucker off like it's made out of nothing more than tissue paper. Tossing the shredded material to the floor, he moves his hands back over his rippling muscles in time with the beats pumping from the speaker.

Beck McCaffery could give Channing Tatum a run for his dancing money.

With the hat remaining low over his face and his dog tags glinting against his tanned skin where they swing around his neck, Beck dances in a circle until his backside draws my full undivided attention.

"Shake it, baby!" I can't help but yell beings it's such a fine one and swiveling right before me.

Beck scowls at me over his shoulder and the man just recreated the first glimpse I ever had of him. Sexy smolder at its finest.

He dances around to face me and saunters over. "Stand up," Beck directs while helping me to my feet. "Turn the music down," he orders.

"Why?"

"You have a story to tell." He settles me into his arms and leads us in a slow dance and arches an eyebrow at me.

"Oh?" Grinning, I reach over and turn the speaker way down.

"Tell me our story."

I love how he always wants a story from me, so I gladly launch into one. "You pushed your way in and sought out the darkness of my soul... Not giving up until filling me completely with light, making me see for the very first time. Life. I see it now. Clearly. Unwritten life that longs to be written with you. I can only see it with you."

Beck reaches over and shuts the song off, but keeps us swaying to a melody only we can feel. We dance until my feet hurt, but I don't want this scene to end. Eventually it does and I have to reluctantly walk him to the door.

"Beck," I whisper and that's all it takes for him to turn and wrap me in his arms

"This is one of the best moments of my life," Beck mumbles against my neck.

A small giggle slips from my lips. "It was pretty amazing."

"No past tense. It is and it's only going to get better."

Chapter Fifteen

Some may say this moment has been in the making for about a year now, but they're wrong. It's been in the making for twenty-nine years, but maybe it's still too soon.

"I can't believe this is what I wanted. Have I lost my ever-loving mind?" I huff out a nervous breath while peeping out the backroom of a fancy bookstore in New York. The place is packed and has a line out the dang door. *What was I thinking?*

It took until another summer has met up with me, but Wild Idea Publishing has just initiated a relaunch of the Breakers Series under the name of Harper Blume. We're celebrating this by releasing a new novel, my debut into the world of contemporary romance.

"Only thing you've lost is your cowardly mentality. I'm proud of you." Beck wraps his arm around my waist and presses a kiss to my forehead.

"Stop with the psychobabble. I'm about to pass out!" I pull in several inhales of his clean soapy scent, willing it to calm me.

He chuckles. "How about a gift to take your mind off this." He reaches over and closes the door.

"I seriously doubt any gift you have could help."

I rest my chin on his chest and look up at him, knowing I just lied. Beck being by my side, reminding me I'm not alone is all the gift I need.

"Close your eyes and we'll see what I can come up with." His turquoise eyes gleam with a secret.

I do as I'm told and feel something heavy meet my finger where it now rests in Beck's warm hand. My eyes flash open and find the most beautiful diamond ring I've ever seen. Princess cut, I think it's called, set in a platinum band.

Stunned by its delicate beauty and the unexpectedness of receiving it, I haul off and punch Beck in the arm with all my might. "You can't do this right before I go out there." I rear back to deliver another punch, but he easily blocks the blow.

"Behave yourself." He presses his lips into a firm line.

"You manipulative jerk. Now I'm going to spend the entire day mentally planning my wedding instead of focusing on the book signing."

"I take that as a yes?" His eyebrow arches.

Slinging my arms around his neck, I jump up and down in excitement. "Yes!"

"Good. Now get out there and be all you can be." He pops my backside with considerable force with his drill sergeant tone infusing each word.

"You're pep-talking me with an Army slogan?"

He shrugs. "It's a good one."

"Enough already. Did you give it to her?" Jack scoots in the room.

I wiggle my finger in front of him.

"'Bout time. Now come on. Your fans have waited long enough to meet you." Jack takes my hand and leads me out of the room and over to a table filled with every book I've written to date. "They're all here to see you, darlin'," he whispers in my ear before releasing my hand.

"I'm here to see them, too." I grin while meeting as many sets of eyes as possible.

I see life now and have no plans of ever going back blind to the vast wonders it offers. And that's the best part about it. It's all there for the taking. The only thing anyone has to do is stop hiding from their fears, surrender it all to God, and claim it like a boss.

"The thief comes only to steal and kill and destroy; I have come that they may have life, and have it to the full." John 10:10 NIV

Epilogue

It wasn't a perfect life, for Lana and Roark were not perfect people. Instead of focusing on the flaws present, they chose to appreciate them, knowing God was doing a work in their lives. It had been a slow process with several rewrites due to circumstances. They both were learning to delete things hindering them and add as many sweet scenes as possible. One day, the couple's life would be written completely. Until then, Lana and Roark promised to live it to the fullest.

"That's it. Time for a break, Mrs. Author."

Before I can retaliate, I find myself tossed over Sergeant Bossy's shoulder and being whisked out of my office.

"Come on, now. We agreed I work five days a week, eight hours a day!" I slap at Beck's butt, but it doesn't slow his long strides one bit. He laid the law down about me living in my office and working an obscene amount of hours, but sometimes a writer just needs to get the words out no matter the time.

"Yes, but you got up in the middle of the night last night and worked for several hours. Time for a break to spend some special time with your husband." He doesn't slow until we are at the foot of our bed, and then playfully tosses me onto the center.

Grinning up at him as I watch his shirt disappear, I say, "Well, how can I resist that." I motion toward him, causing Beck's incredible grin to join mine.

The next hour or so is quite special…

"What are you laughing at?" I mutter, half asleep.

"You were snoring."

"Was not." I snuggle closer and feel Beck's arms tighten around me. *Divine.*

"Okay, go back to sleep."

"How long have I been out?"

"About an hour."

"Ugh. Why'd you let me sleep for that long?" I try rubbing the sleep from my eyes.

"You needed the rest. Plus, I've been enjoying watching you drool all over my chest." He chuckles quietly.

I use the blanket to mop up my mess, realizing I was more exhausted than I thought. My husband always knows, though. After I dry his chest, I snuggle back down and revel in his warmth and soapy scent. A while back I did some internet research on pheromones and chemical reactions to try to make some sense as to why Beck's scent drives me crazy in such a good way. Some say such reactions are only found in animals, but I beg to differ. Never has soap had this effect on me until meeting this amazing man. I think it was all God. He wanted to make sure I was so drawn to Beck, I wouldn't be able to run away. It worked, that's for sure.

"You love women drooling over you," I tease and

take a deep inhale of my most favorite smell in the entire world—my husband.

"Only one woman. Don't mistake me for Jack."

"Ah, but he's not so bad anymore. There are only a few women who seem to be drooling over him at church nowadays."

"I need to warn them about his wicked mouth." Beck snorts.

We like to tease Jack about his wicked mouth, but the man has the purest of hearts. It didn't take long after I gave my life over to God that Jack found it appealing enough to do the same. He has closed his Italian restaurant every Sunday for the past one and a half years, so that our church family can meet there. I've lost count of how many meals he's had waiting for everyone at the end of services. This Sunday will be the last meeting at the restaurant. It will be bittersweet.

I trace the smooth, black lines of the harp tattooed over Beck's heart and ask, "Have the pews been delivered yet?"

"Not until this afternoon. Jack is going to meet me over there and help install them."

"That's great."

"Yeah. It's even greater that someone's anonymous donation funded the entire rebuild of Oceanside." Beck squeezes me a little tighter for emphasis, but I ignore it.

I know that he knows the donation came from my bloated bank account, but we don't acknowledge it. I've been beyond blessed, so that I can bless others.

It's also led me to fund a charity for young women struggling with any type of addiction, whether it is food and the eating disorders that come along with it, substance abuse, sexual, or even shopping. A group of women from church help out with it and it's become nationally recognized. Yes, I use any book event to plug it, but that's a perk to this newfound fame. Admittedly, it's helped me stay sober as well. A few chapters have been difficult, but keeping my focus in the right place and the support of my loved ones has helped.

"I'm gonna grab a quick shower and go with you." I untangle myself from his arms and the sheets, but not before Beck pulls me back for one more kiss.

"I love you," he whispers against my lips.

"And I love you," I whisper right back.

After a little more kissing, I head to the shower with the last few years swirling around in my head. One of the most important lessons I've finally grasped is forgiveness and letting things go. My love for internet searches led me to look up the definition of opinion one day while contemplating how negative I felt against my childhood church.

Opinion is a view or judgment formed in the mind about a particular matter.

We all have an opinion, even though it may not line up with everyone else's. Funny how my transformation has changed my opinion. I've visited my parents and attended church with them several times recently. I go to church to praise God nowadays and not to nitpick His people to death. Sure, some are the same as they ever were, but now I just feel sorry for them. They're cheating themselves out of a sweet relationship with God by focusing on their rituals. Here's praying they change their opinion someday soon.

As for me, I'm gonna keep my focus on God and allow Him to pen the rest of my unwritten life the way He sees fit.

Life Unwritten Playlist

"Way Down We Go" by Kaleo
"Sober" by P!nk
"When I'm With You" by Citizen Way
"Perfect" by P!nk
"Flowers in Your Hair" by The Lumineers
"Magnify" by We Are Messengers
"Welcome to Your Life" by Grouplove
"Send the Rain" by Aaron Butler
"Brand New" by Ben Rector
"Live Like You're Loved" by Hawk Nelson

ABOUT THE AUTHOR

Bestselling author T.I. Lowe sees herself as an ordinary country girl who loves to tell extraordinary stories. She knows she's just getting started and has many more stories to tell. A wife and mother and active in her church community, she resides in coastal South Carolina with her family.

For a complete list of Lowe's published books, biography, upcoming events, and other information, visit http://www.tilowe.com/ and be sure to check out her blog, COFFEE CUP, while you're there!

She loves to connect with her reading friends.

ti.lowe@yahoo.com

https://www.facebook.com/T.I.Lowe/

Printed in Great Britain
by Amazon

57286728R00148